Tempest and the Infinite Variations

A Shiloh Tempest novel: the prequel

David Hunter

Debbie,
A tall lawyer friend told me you like my books, I hope you enjoy my latest one.

David Hunter
1/19/17

Tempest and the Infinite Variations

Printed in the United States of America.

Oconee Spirit Press, Waverly, TN www.oconeespirit.com

978-0-9859107-4-7

Library of Congress Cataloging-in-Publication Data

Hunter, David. Tempest and the Infinite Variables.

p.cm.

1.Police – Tennessee - Fiction. 2. Knoxville (Tenn.) – Fiction. 3. Tempest, Shiloh (Fictitious character).

The text paper is SFI certified. The Sustainable Forestry Initiative® program promotes sustainable forest management.

Cover design by Dead Center
Cover image © Kozorez Vladislav | Shutterstock.com

To Cheryl, once again...

ONE

There are only three basic plots: Individuals in conflict with other individuals; individuals in conflict with the natural forces of the universe, or God, if you prefer; and individuals in conflict with themselves.

Shelia Pritchard, my high school English teacher, first told me this when I was a senior in the Powell High Class of 1965. I tried to argue with her because I'd read somewhere that there were seven. Now I know that some so-called experts list as many as thirty-six. Also, I was in love with her and wanted very much to impress her with my skills as a literary maven.

"No," Shelia was firm about it. "There are infinite variations, but only three basic plots." She was a freckled woman, petite, dark-haired, green-eyed and only eight years older than I was at seventeen. Our future happiness was within the realm of adolescent possibility.

"What about the individual against society?" I said.

"It's covered under 'individuals against other individuals.' Society is not a monolithic entity; it's composed of individuals."

"What about Moby Dick?" I asked her.

"It's covered under 'individuals in conflict with the forces of nature' or 'individuals in conflict with other individuals.' I'd go with the first, but Ahab was an individual and the white whale was also an individual as well as a force of nature."

Before I could answer, Jeannette Ripley came to the classroom door looking for me. I was also in love with her and she was also petite and dark-haired, but with brown eyes. Unlike Sheila Pritchard, Jeannette would go parking with me behind Bell's Camp Ground Methodist Church for intimate make out sessions.

Shelia and I never resumed the conversation but I never forgot it either. Forty years later when I found out she had died of cancer, I remembered the day as if it had happened yesterday. There are only three basic plots with infinite variations.

TWO

"Your nurse says she caught you smoking a cigarette this morning. Aside from the damage to your heart and arteries, it's dangerous to smoke around oxygen. How did you get the cigarettes?"

Doctor Olsen is tall and rangy. When I first started seeing him, his hair was black and he always looked as if he needed a shave, even early in the morning. Now his hair is streaked with silver and so is the beard he's been wearing for ten years. He has made a valiant effort to keep me alive.

"It's not exactly a maximum security ward, John."

"So one of your friends brought them to you?"

"Doctor, I never reveal my sources." The truth was, I had two packs in my jacket pocket when I was brought in, and the staff had hung it up in the locker with my shirt and pants. If I told the truth, however, they would take the second pack.

"We need to talk about putting in the defibrillator."

"All right, we can talk about it."

"If we don't do it, it's just a matter of time until you die."

"It's just a matter of time until I die, anyway, John."

"If you'll stop smoking and let me put the defibrillator in, you can live another twenty years. The technology keeps improving."

"That would take me almost all the way to eighty. There's hardly anything left now that I still enjoy. What will I have at eighty?"

"Why didn't you just *leave* when you first came around and save everyone the trouble of stabilizing you?" Doctor Olson had let his facade slip and the frustration showed momentarily. That doesn't happen often.

"Because I'd just pass out again and end up back in the emergency room with people pounding my chest with electric paddles."

"Are you going to let me implant the defibrillator?" Doctor Olson asked with a sigh and a wry smile. Over twenty years, we've worked out a rapport of sorts, a friendship, even. He tries to save me and I resist. So far, he still has the upper hand.

"I need to think about it, John."

"Don't take too long. We need the bed for someone who really *wants* to live."

"I'll keep that in mind, Doctor."

As Olson was leaving, he passed my morning shift nurse, Nurse Solly, making her first of many daily entrances.

"How are we today, Mister Tempest?"

Nurse Solly is perhaps twenty-five, tall, bespectacled — leaving me to wonder if she can't wear contact lenses or afford eye surgery or if she is merely confident as herself — blond and Reubenesque. Not a runway model body type, but the kind of body most men really want. Marilyn Monroe, not Kate Moss.

I allow her to get away with speaking in the plural — even though I agree with Mark Twain that only royalty and people with tapeworms should do so — because I like her and because I find her attractive, despite the fact that my erotic impulses no longer seem to reach the intended body part, but are more like what I've read about the sensation of a shadow limb after an amputation. She isn't my type, which is exotic. But male lust is not selective.

"Are you here to prod, poke and torture my decrepit body, or just here for a social visit, Nurse Solly?"

"You're far from decrepit, Mister Tempest. Some would say you're in the prime of life."

"Your mother perhaps, Nurse Solly?"

"No, actually my mother is into tall, blond men. I like the rugged adventurous type myself. Have you tested your blood sugar this morning?"

"No, but it's too high. It always is."

"Well, if you won't do it, I suppose I'd better." She picked up the electronic meter from my bedside table and put in a test strip, then leaned over and took my hand. Her nails were clipped and uncolored and the smell of honeysuckle wafted under my nose. There was a minor sting as she pierced my finger.

"You know, don't you, that you're going to end up on insulin if you don't get your blood sugar under control. Diabetes can do a lot of nerve damage."

"It already has," I replied as she teased a drop of blood onto the test strip. "Besides, it's a contest between diabetes and my heart as to which will kill me first."

"The night nurse made a notation on your chart that she caught you in the bathroom smoking a cigarette last night."

"Not the first time I've been caught misbehaving in a bathroom, Nurse Solly. It probably won't be the last." The meter beeped and she looked at it.

"It's one-forty-nine," he said. "Not extremely high, but too high."

"Actually, that's pretty good for me."

"I know you're not really a cynic," she said, her cheeks pinking up. "I've read two of your books and I feel like I know you. Why do you put so much effort into pretending?"

"Which two?" I asked.

"*God's Vagabonds* and *The Underbelly*."

"Read *The Salvation of David Sage* and see if you still think I'm not a cynic, Nurse Solly."

"I didn't know about that one." She leaned over to fluff my pillow and I inhaled essence of woman with a honeysuckle tinge.

"It wasn't a bestseller. I changed directions and the reading public never allows that. The public wants the same book over and over, with only the names of places and people changed. I gave them what they wanted after the flop. I'm no better than a common whore."

"You are such a drama queen sometimes, Mister Tempest. I was an English literature major before I switched to nursing. In a world of people who want be authors, there are many people who would give up body parts to do what you've already done."

"Ah, an English lit major. Are you familiar with Dylan Thomas, then?"

"I've read some of his work."

"*Though wise men at their end know dark is right, because their words had forked no lightning, they do not go gentle into that good night.*" Nurse Solly, because my words have forked no lightning, I do not intend to go gently. I'll go out kicking and screaming."

"Refusing medical treatment and advice that would prolong your life seems just the opposite of 'raging at the dying of the light' to me."

Before I could respond, she went on: "You haven't filled out your lunch menu request, Mister Tempest."

"It doesn't matter. They have me on a diabetic *and* heart-healthy menu. Whatever they give me will be tasteless."

"You do insist on being a problem patient, don't you?"

She turned and walked out of the room and even in the modified surgical scrubs that nurses wear these days, her buttocks reminded me of a boa constrictor writhing inside a pillow case. No man ever stops looking, no matter how old or impotent.

"Mister Tempest?"

The priest was a man of medium height and broad shoulders, with a shiny, bald head with short-cropped gray hair on the sides, and what would have been called "apple cheeks" in a more prosaic time. I would view them as an overfondness for alcohol. He stood at the door as if hesitant to enter.

"Yes?"

"I'm Father Fleming. I know it's late, but I wondered if I might speak with you a few minutes – if you're not too busy."

"Come in. My social calendar isn't full at the moment. Have a seat."

"The sisters and nurses are all excited to have a celebrity on the floor," Father Fleming said, pulling up a chair by my bed. He grimaced with what was meant to be a conspiratorial smile to let me know he was above anything so crass as celebrity worship.

"They must be hard up for celebrities, Father."

"Well, you *are* a best-selling author."

"I once was. My last bestseller was twelve years ago. I've had a dry spell since then. How can I help you, Father?"

"I try to keep up with my pastoral duties, and I know you're a Roman Catholic," he said, shifting in the uncomfortable straightback chair.

"I'm a lapsed Catholic – an orthodox agnostic, Father."

"Well, many great writers, such as T.S. Elliot and C.S. Lewis, spent time in the wilderness of agnosticism. And I've read *The Salvation of David Sage*, in which you definitely showed a familiarity with theological issues, particularly salvation."

"I'm surprised, Father, that you mention me in the same sentence with two literary giants, and that you've read a book that was remaindered out the first year. But if you'll recall, I left the question of God hanging in the last chapter."

"Ah yes, there was ambiguity. But nobody wanders so far they can't get back to God."

"Suppose God doesn't exist, Father?"

"Mister Tempest, just look around. Does the universe look like an accident to you?"

"Of course it doesn't *look* like an accident. We belong to a species that seeks out patterns, Father."

"Mister Tempest, that magnificent brain of yours should be evidence enough of creation."

"It *is* magnificent, Father. But did God create the brain or did the brain create God while looking for a pattern?"

"Well, obviously *I* believe in a creator, Mister Tempest."

"That's very comforting, I know from my childhood. But for me, it only moves the question back a step. If God is the watchmaker, who made God, Father Fleming?"

"You're a clever man, Mister Tempest. Perhaps we can talk later." Obviously, Father Fleming had not come prepared.

"Assuming I'm still here, Father Fleming, you'd be most welcome – if you don't try to leave a pamphlet that says 'Accept my loving God or he'll send you to Hell' – like the Baptist who came through yesterday. Otherwise, we can talk."

"We don't use those kinds of pamphlets these days. I suppose you'd be more comfortable if I prayed for you at another location?" the priest said.

"Where you pray shouldn't matter to an omniscient, omnipresent and omnipotent God, so somewhere else would be more comfortable for both of us."

It seemed likely Father Fleming would do some boning up before returning. But he never did come back.

THREE

There's always a feeling of disorientation when I wake up in a hospital room. It doesn't happen in hotels, but it always happens in hospital rooms. Maybe it's the smell of disinfectant or the quiet beeping and hissing of machines.

"Good morning, sleepyhead. I was about to leave."

The Latina beauty — Jennifer Mendoza, who had arrived in the U.S.A by way of Colombia — sitting by my bed was my live-in compañera for twenty years. I've been told that Mendoza was a Basque root that means "mountains," or "cold mountains." Her native tongue was Castilian. I'm too linguistically ignorant to understand, but I have been assured that Castilian is very different from the Spanish spoken in the New World.

I first noticed her because she looked like Madeline Stowe, whom I first saw in a cop movie with Richard Dreyfus and Emilio Estevez. It was called *Stakeout.* Jennifer was twenty at the time, studying political science in preparation for law school, and I was thirty-eight and a sergeant at the sheriff's department.

"Why are you up so early?" I asked.

"I have to be in federal court this morning to debate how my client ended up with two kilos of cocaine he says he didn't know about."

"Good luck."

"I'll need it," she said, pushing a strand of raven hair from her face. It was still as anthracite black as the day I met her. "Here's the book you asked me to pick up at your apartment. You need a maid, though I suppose she'd seem out of place in that dump where you live now."

"James Agee and Leslie Garrett lived in that neighborhood. It's just a place to sleep and work."

"John called me yesterday. He's worried about you."

"Why is my cardiologist calling *you?*" I sounded sharper than I had intended, but she chose to ignore my tone.

"For the same reason I'm here this morning – we slept together for twenty years, and I was the one he came out and talked to every time you had surgery."

"That's only because you won't be reasonable and move on with your life."

"I'm not ready to move on."

"We've been through this, Jennifer. You had a whole man, you're still young and beautiful, and I'm old and used up. Everything important that I ever was is in the past and you need to move into the future."

"You're such a bullshit artist. You're *still* everything that was important to me when I moved in with you. Sexual athletics are important to you, not to me!"

Nurse Solly walked through the door just in time to catch Jennifer's last statement. "I'm sorry… didn't know you had company." She made a quick exit.

"Is the book for her?" Jennifer asked. "She's quite beautiful in a school-marm sort of way."

"Yes, the book is for her. Yes, she's beautiful, but we both know that's a matter of aesthetics for me these days, with no practical application."

"Don't get defensive, Detective. I know she's not your type, but that doesn't mean you aren't *her* type."

"Never saw myself as a father figure," I said.

"Have you called Sam to congratulate him on being sworn in as the new sheriff? He's been trying to call you."

"He may have been trying to call me here. I've had the phone shut off. And no, I haven't called to congratulate him. I'm sure everyone he's known in twenty-eight years of law enforcement is calling him, angling for a job."

"Most of them didn't turn keys with him when they worked together in the jail as rookies. You two have a lot of history."

"Maybe I'll call him this afternoon."

"You *should*. I'm going to get out of here and let that embarrassed nurse do whatever she needs to do." She kissed me lightly on the cheek and left behind the faint, familiar odor of orange blossoms. At such moments, I miss being with her so much I want to cry.

I took a drag off my cigarette, then a sip of fresh cafeteria coffee and leaned back on the bench in the grassy area where visitors could come and smoke, one of the few places on the grounds where pariahs can still gather to indulge their sin.

While I was waiting for Nurse Solly to return, someone had apparently coded, which is hospital jargon for 'serious trouble.' While the staff was running up and down the hallway pushing carts, I put on my robe and took a walk.

I knew my excursion wouldn't last long, but the morning sun felt good. A young security officer had already dashed out the nearby door, headed for the bus stop at the main entrance to the hospital. It was good thinking on his part, since I had no vehicle with me.

When the officer came back, I was just putting out my second cigarette. He looked to be in his mid-twenties and appeared very professional. I took him for a man on the short list to be hired at the Knoxville Police Department or the sheriff's department – perhaps a military veteran making do with security work until he could fulfill his dream. He stopped in front of me.

"Mister Tempest, you've created a lot of commotion," he said. There was a bead of sweat on his forehead. He took his portable radio from a belt clip. "Unit five, I have Mister Tempest in the east smoking area."

"Do we know each other, Officer…" I looked at his name tag… "White?"

"*Most* people in law enforcement know you, Mister Tempest. We're to wait here until they bring a wheelchair."

"I hadn't intended to go anywhere else, Officer White. Have a seat; you look like you've overexerted yourself."

"If it's all the same to you, I'll stand." He was a big man, maybe six-three, a good eight or nine inches taller than me.

"Nice looking leather," I said. The basket weave design was gleaming all over. "Is that Glock a .40 caliber or 9 millimeter?"

"It's .40 caliber," he replied. "What do you carry?"

"When I bother these days, I still carry my baby Glock, 9 millimeter."

"That's a good weapon. Doesn't have the stopping power of a 40 caliber, though."

Ask a cop about his weapon and he will talk forever. We were still talking when Nurse Solly came out the door followed by an orderly with a wheelchair. She stood in front of me, hands on her ample, curvaceous hips.

"Mister Tempest, you have risked your life and my reputation by disappearing from your room!"

"Your *reputation*, Nurse Solly?"

"I take great pride in taking good care of my patients. I certainly can't take care of you if I don't know where you are."

It was a quiet ride to the elevator and back up to the cardiology ward. In my room, she pointed to the bed without speaking and I sat down without argument. She undressed me like a child. By the time she had my monitoring equipment back in place she seemed a little calmer.

"I have a present for you, Nurse Solly. It's in the drawer of my little bedside table. I had Jennifer bring it this morning."

She opened the drawer and took out a copy of *The Salvation of David Sage*, and dimpled up in the manner of girls and very young women, despite trying to stay angry and stern.

"Is Jennifer your wife?" She opened the book and saw that I had inscribed it *To Nurse Solly, who tells me what to do*, then smiled.

"No. We were together twenty years, but we're apart now."

"If you behave with her the way you've behaved here, I can understand why she left you. I need your word you won't do this to me again."

"You have my word." *There are two other shifts if I need another walk.*

"Shiloh Tempest, they tell me you took unauthorized leave this morning," said Sam Renfro, the new county sheriff, who had been selected by county commission and sworn in when the previous sheriff was indicted for taking rather large bribes. He had charged in without warning and started talking without preliminaries.

Sam is five-eleven, slim to chunky, depending on when you see him. Fiftyish and boyish despite his years, he was wearing a tailored tan suit and saddle oxford shoes, brown and tan. He had a manila envelope under his arm.

"I also had a 'no visitors' order, except for Jennifer, but it doesn't seem to be working. Nice shoes, Sammy."

"Do you have any idea how big a set of balls it takes for a man to wear a pair of shoes like these around cops?" He put the manila envelope on the bedside table, pulled up the chair and straddled it like a horse with the back in front of him.

"I'm sad you didn't call and congratulate me. Of course, I've heard from every sonofabitch I ever met in the last thirty years and *everybody* wants something."

"That's what I figured. I was going to call you today, but I see Jennifer has already sent you around to tell me why I need to do what my doctor says."

"She told me you were here when I called, but that's all. What that woman sees in you, I'll never know. I wish she'd drop you. I'd snap her up in a minute. Then, when the next election comes in three years, they'd be running pictures of me and my beautiful Latina lawyer wife on the society pages."

Sam's hair was expertly coiffed and pushed back. There has always been a chameleon quality about him. When we worked narcotics, he once posed as a drug dealer and when someone took an outlaw biker to meet him, the biker said he wouldn't deal with such a "nasty-looking bastard."

"What's in the manila envelope, Sam?"

"It's just something I wanted to get your slant on – the Cynthia Quinn case. The press has already started asking me questions about it."

"Yeah, I've seen her uncle and aunt on television, demanding justice."

"Well, they *did* raise her. I guess I can understand how they feel. She's been dead two years and we don't have a good suspect yet. Will you look at it for me? It's just the basics and detective's summary."

"Sam, I had a good run as a cop and a pretty good run as an author after my heart started going bad. I don't need your damned charity work because Jennifer thinks I need a *purpose!* Besides, I never worked homicide."

"Hoss, I'm not in the charity business. I brought you the case because we're at a dead-end. I'm already looking at what the case will do to me when I run for reelection.

"I know you *never* worked homicide, but you kept up with forensics and the homicide dicks used to ask for your opinion. Besides, I didn't figure out whoddunit until the last page of your first novel. Hell, son, you *think* like a murderer."

"All right, Sam. Leave the file and I'll take a look at it."

"I knew you'd come through. Should you be interested, I can find a way to bring you back to the department temporarily."

"It's not likely, Sam."

Is there anything I can get for you before I leave?"

"Cigarettes would be nice. Nurse Solly took my last pack and they're watching me like a hawk."

"You're asking a man who has been your friend for almost thirty years, a man who doesn't even smoke, to smuggle a harmful substance into a hospital room?"

"That was the request."

"Camel filters, right?"

"Preferably."

He reached into his coat pocket and tossed me two packs of Camel filters. "Hoss, do a better job of hiding these." He was gone before I could say anything. He always leaves a room that way.

FOUR

When Doctor Olsen came in the next morning, I was still reading the Cynthia Quinn case file. I had been poring over it most of the night. It was a classic locked room murder mystery – an individual in conflict with at least one other individual, and most likely an individual in conflict with himself.

"Shiloh, we need to talk about putting in the defibrillator. The insurance company won't let me keep you any longer and we need the bed."

"Schedule the surgery, John."

"Now I suspect you have some kind of romantic idea about defying the universe and God but... did you say *schedule* the surgery?"

"As soon as possible."

"Do you want to discuss the possible complications? Considering your condition, they're fairly minimal, but you need to be informed." Conflicting emotions played across his bearded face as ethics made him get into things he didn't really want to say.

"John, I know what the complication will be if I *don't* have it. I'll die soon; isn't that what you've been telling me?"

"Yes, but..." He shook his head. "All right, I'll schedule it. You're a puzzle inside a riddle wrapped in an enigma, Shiloh."

"That's what Winston Churchill said about Russian foreign policy, John. But a thing is only mysterious if you don't know all the facts. Once you understand the basic plot, it all makes sense."

The thing they implanted in my body the next day is technically called an *implanted pacer cardioverter defibrillator* or PCD. It is a multipurpose little device. It sends out small, swift electrical impulses over wires fed into the heart to set the pace for tachycardia, excessively fast heart rate -- and bradycardia, a too-slow heart rate-- or a stronger impulse when the pacing feature doesn't restore a regular heartbeat.

In my particular case, it is there to give a high-energy shock to restart my heart if it detects fibrillation, which is a quivering that can quickly cause death because no blood is actually being pumped. Think of a miniature version of the paddles you see television doctors slap on a patient's chest.

Even stoned on sedatives, it felt like being punched in the heart by a martial arts expert when they tweaked the device after it was implanted to make sure it was working properly. The wires are run in through arteries to the heart and the actual device hardly makes a bump under my stomach muscles.

The PCD can be tested with a scanner, and the data can even be transmitted by phone. True, the batteries have to be changed periodically but that time is measured in five to eight year cycles now as battery technology improves. I've never worried about *anything* five years down the road.

When I opened my eyes again after the procedure was over, Jennifer was sitting by the bed.

"We have to stop meeting like this, Counselor," I said.

"That's true; my boyfriend carries a weapon and it could lead to serious problems. Why did I have to find out from your cardiologist that you had decided to let him put in the defibrillator?"

"Well, you were the one who sent my friend Sheriff Renfro over to give me a purpose for living. I assumed you and Sam and John were keeping each other informed."

"John did call me, but I didn't talk to Sam about what was going on, except to tell him you were here when he called for you."

"Sure you did. The timing was perfect. He waltzes in here with a murder mystery to solve just at the moment you and John are trying to talk me into having the defibrillator installed."

"Tempest, lying to you was never among the problems we had. Maybe the timing came from elsewhere."

"Oh yeah.'He-who-sees-every-sparrow fall,' perhaps?"

"There was a time when you believed that."

"There was a time when I believed in Santa Claus, but when I got the cheap version of the Daisy air-rifle instead of the deluxe Red Ryder edition, I figured out that Santa was my bargain-hunting father. But if you say you didn't call Sam, I believe you."

"That's very gracious of you, Tempest." I saw tears about to overflow her brown eyes and wondered for the thousandth time why a woman like her had not only fallen in love with me but continued to love me as my body began to fail one organ at a time. She only called me by my last name when she was upset.

"I jump to conclusions. I'm sorry. It's a bad trait in an investigator and a human being in general."

"They're cutting you loose in the morning. John left the operator's manual for your PCD. I never expected to have a man with an operator's manual."

"You were the right person to get it. You know I never read the instructions. That's why we spent a Christmas Eve without power or lights when I decided to install the smoke detector my mother gave us and ran a screw through the copper water pipe and the main electrical line in that dinky basement apartment on Atlantic."

"John says you'll need watching for a few days. Why don't I take some vacation and you stay at our house until you're back on your feet."

"It isn't *our* house, Jennifer. I signed it over to you, and you shouldn't be spending your time watching over a degenerating old man."

"Don't be an ass about it, Tempest. I have a guest bedroom and there could still be complications. Besides, your grandfather may have been old at fifty-nine, but sixty is the new forty today."

"All right, Jen. I'll stay at your house for a few days. But there will be no fetching and hovering and no bringing me coffee."

"When did I ever do that, Shiloh? I'll be here in the morning. I have to get to court on a client who decided to take a shot at a black bear with a .25 caliber pistol in the Smoky Mountains National Park."

"I presume you'll be asking for mercy because he was disabled by the bear?"

"No, his aim was no better than his judgment." She kissed me on the cheek and turned to leave.

That morning she was wearing a simply cut business suit but it still showed her dynamite figure to good advantage. As she walked away, that mane of raven hair falling down her back, I felt a sexual stirring.

Impotence, it used to be called in less open times. Now it's *erectile dysfunction* and presidential candidates discuss it. How I had handled it was a disappointment, even to me.

I had always considered myself a rational, thinking man, whose manhood was not centered in his penis. But I was not prepared at all when it began to happen to me — and I didn't take it lying down, figuratively speaking, of course.

I visited a urologist, tried each new pill and even the horrible vacuum pump system. When they all failed, I took my file and saw Mike Bolander, a psychologist I knew from the police academy. He was upfront about it.

"Shiloh, you have blocked arteries, you take at least six medications that can affect performance and you have diabetes, which damages nerves. Your equipment should have quit working years ago for those reasons alone.

"The fact that you can still get an erection tells me that there may be some emotional blockage. You think you'll fail, you do fail and it becomes a self-fulfilling prophecy.

"I could refer you to a sexual surrogate — but you've refused to discuss it. So my advice is that you can learn to make love *without* using your penis. Thousands of men do for various reasons. When I talked to Jennifer, she indicated that the latter suggestion is fine with her."

And I knew it *was* fine with Jennifer. She had told me often enough. In the end, however, I did the only thing an honorable medieval man could have done. I moved out so that my Jennifer could have a new life with another man who was sexually whole.

FIVE

"It's good to see you back at work, Shiloh. What does Jennifer think about it?" Sam Renfro leaned back in his chair and surveyed me from across the half-acre desk his predecessor had installed. There were no police knickknacks on the desk, just a picture of Sam's father who had been a captain at the Knoxville Police Department.

"She couldn't be happier, Sam. When you showed up with the Cynthia Quinn file, I was debating whether or not to let them put in this little device that turned me into a bionic man."

"What was the debate about? It's my understanding that it's a matter of life or death when they actually use those things. You don't have a death wish, do you, Shiloh? There were some who said you did when you worked the streets."

"I don't think so, Sam. There was a lot in play."

"Fair enough. I've put you on the books as a consultant at a lieutenant's grade, so it doesn't screw up your pension. You can make twenty-five grand before they start screaming. Any travel expenses will go on a credit card they'll issue you in finance." He stood up from his thousand dollar plush leather chair, also purchased by his predecessor.

"Let's go get you an ID card and a new picture, and I'll introduce you to your crew. You can use the lieutenant's badge you kept at retirement. Training tells me you've stayed qualified with your handgun."

"That I have done, Sam, with my Glock 26 and my S&W bodyguard."

"Your Glock will do for the time being," Sam said.

Several old-timers stopped me and shook my hand, but they were in the minority. I had been gone twelve years and that's a long time in police work. With a fresh ID card in my pocket, we got on the elevator and went down to the sub-level of the City-County building.

"The two detectives that have been assigned to this case since it happened two years ago are in a separate room from everyone else, mostly because they have ten filing cabinets already devoted to this one case."

"Is the family already on your back about airing the case on that national television show?" I asked.

"Yeah, they started calling the day I was sworn in. I glanced at the file I left with you at the hospital and decided it wasn't a good idea. You may disagree after you talk to the detectives. If you do, we'll discuss it."

As soon as we walked into the cluttered office, I saw how things were going to shake out with the two detectives — but I had expected it. Both were as close to sullenness as they dared to be while talking to their boss.

"Detective John Freed and Detective Al Reagan, this is Lieutenant Shiloh Tempest. I told you he might be joining us for a while, and he was good enough to accept my invitation. You will cooperate in every way. He didn't fall off the last load of turnips that came through. He's cop to the bone. We clear?"

"You got it, Sheriff," Freed said. He was a redhead, of the freckled and carrot top variety, a man in his late twenties, with a voice that was almost contralto. His nose came down into a slope that would have impressed Bob Hope.

His partner, Reagan, was a big man, husky, going to fat, who looked as if he might have a Latin or Cherokee grandparent. He was maybe forty, wearing rimless glasses, with dark thinning hair that was cropped close to the scalp, and and he was sporting a shoulder holster, which is frowned upon by training officers because of what they consider clumsiness and below speed performance, and usually indicates a cop with a streak of individualism.

"You guys get to know each other," the Sheriff said, then left in his usual abrupt manner.

After Sam left, the room fell quiet and both men appeared busy again with whatever they were doing before we came in. I knew it was for my benefit. They were working a cold case and the work is in spurts, not steady. I looked at the large moveable bulletin board with 8x10 crime scene photos, most of which I had already seen. There was also a composite drawing of the suspect and the FBI profile posted there.

"Is this my desk?" I asked.

"Yeah, that's yours, *Lieutenant*," Freed answered.

"All right, gentlemen, we're going to cut the dogs-sniffing-asses short because I'm not good at role playing *or* games." I had their attention.

"I know the two of you resent having me here. It's been *your* case for two years. You think if there was anything else to know, you'd know it. I'm a relic from the past and a celebrity, who thinks more highly of himself than he ought to, as far as you're concerned.

"I'd feel the same way in your shoes. But the Sheriff has given me a job to do and I'm going to do it, with or without your help. If you can't abide my presence, the sheriff will reassign you — in which case you will look incompetent, should I solve it.

"Personally, I think it's a win-win situation for the two of you. If by chance we solve the case because I see something with fresh eyes, *you* get the credit. If not, you get to laugh your asses off at the sick old man who thinks he's still a cop.

"Now, I'm going to haul my decrepit body to the john and take a leak, maybe find a cup of coffee. I want two things when I get back. I want my desk cleaned off and facing the door, because I don't trust anybody behind my back. And I want the two of you to be ready to summarize this case."

They were looking at each other as I left the room, reassessing the situation.

In the restroom, I took a leak and washed my hands. In the mirror that ran the length of the wall, I took a close look at myself and saw a short man who looked a lot like my father when he wore a suit and tie on Sunday.

The man in the mirror was thirty pounds overweight, broad through the shoulders and had almost no neck. His hair, always a nondescript brown, was cut almost military short and was becoming more silver by the month. His coat was a 48 short, his waist was larger than the inseam of his off-the-rack slacks from J.C. Penny, his shirt was plaid and his tie, as always, was a solid color to match the basic plaid. He didn't look sick and never really had. But he looked tired, very tired.

The restroom door swung open and a tall, husky man with curly dark hair, also streaked with silver, walked in. He carried himself erect like a soldier, though I knew he'd never served in the military at all — a man caught between Vietnam and the first Gulf War in age.

"I *thought* I saw you with the Sheriff. Still hanging out with the big dogs while other people do the grunt work." He went to the urinal, unzipped his pants and began to relieve himself.

"And I see your upper lip still doesn't move when you talk, Captain Rosenbaum. Or is it Assistant Chief Rosenbaum? I concede you're an expert on the fine art of kissing the proper ass."

"It's *chief* of detectives now, and the two detectives assigned to you still work for me." He turned, zipping his pants. Then he walked to the sink and washed his hands.

"Until the first time you get in my way, Timmy. Nice to see you again." I left him drying his hands.

Back in the cluttered office, I found there had been a visible attitude shift.

"I got you a cuppa joe, Lieutenant," Al Reagan said, in a voice that was deep and gravely, as if he had been shouting or had a sore throat. "I didn't know how you drink it, so I brought a pack of creamer and sugar. We cleaned off your desk. If you want more coffee, they keep a fresh pot around in major crimes. Everybody tosses in a buck every now and then."

"I appreciate that." I took a seat at my new desk. It was as warm as things would get for a while. I had to earn my bones. They had cleared my desk and brought coffee, but had also let me know it was a favor because they were detectives and didn't fetch coffee for anybody.

"Where do you want us to start?" Freed asked.

"Walk me through from the beginning. I've read your notes, but I want to hear it the way you saw it."

Reagan pulled the bulletin board to an angle where I could clearly see it and begin to speak. "The call came in at 2107 and the response time was eight minutes. The first officer on the scene met Cynthia Quinn's roommate in front of the apartment building — Robert Swenson, age twenty-six.

"He was badly cut and bleeding with wounds the ER doctor said couldn't have been self-inflicted." He pointed to a picture of the man lying on a gurney with several stab wounds at the emergency room before he was stitched up. He was a slight young man, very little muscle.

"The first officer called for backup and an ambulance, then found the girl here in the foyer of the apartment building — here in this photo — where she had stumbled from the apartment and fallen after the roommate ran for help. Bad as they were, the girl would have survived the wounds if help had arrived a few minutes earlier. She bled out. There were two dozen stab wounds. It was personal."

Reagan pointed to the picture of Cynthia Quinn on the slab in the medical examiner's office. She look like a waif and had a child-like appearance at twenty-three, thin and pale with tiny breasts and short strawberry blonde hair, cut in what I had always thought of as a "pixie" cut. I knew from the coroner's report that she had been stabbed with so much force that the butcher knife had bent.

I swallowed hard, trying not to be obvious, and remembered why I had never worked homicide.

Freed picked up the narrative, all but warbling. His voice would take some getting used to. "The roommate said the victim had gone to her room and closed the door about two hours earlier, and he was in his room reading with the door also closed, when he first heard a commotion.

"He says he paid no attention at first because Quinn was prone to sleep-walking and nightmares. He says he got up and opened his door and the suspect was backing out of the victim's room. The lights were off and the roommate says he didn't get an exceptionally good look at the guy before he was suddenly being stabbed the first time.

"According to the roommate, the suspect pushed him back on to the bed in his own room, repeatedly stabbing him, until something seemed to distract him — at which point he ran out of the bedroom, went through the kitchen and out the back door.

"Svenson says the back door was locked and the blood smears bear out his story. He also says the front door was locked — both the deadbolt and the regular door lock — when he ran out for help. He says Quinn always threw the deadbolt even when she wasn't home alone, but both locks opened with the same key.

"The girl got up after Svenson left, staggered from the apartment and collapsed in the foyer, near the front door. Cynthia fought like a tiger."

"We really liked the roommate for the killing, in spite of his defensive injuries, until the DNA results came back. Both the victim and the roommate's blood were on the knife but there was blood from a third party, a male, on the knife and the same person left a blood smear on the kitchen door on the way out, as well some drip spatters on the sidewalk."

"You two satisfied that the roommate is in the clear?" I asked. They immediately glanced at each other, as if maybe I wasn't a complete waste of time.

"We don't think he killed her, "Reagan said. "But we think he knows more than he's telling us — like maybe he's too afraid of the killer to talk."

"Did you put him on the box during the initial investigation?" They glanced at each other again.

"Yeah, we did, but there was a bad glitch, you might say," Reagan said. "We were gonna call our regular lie detector guy, but Chief Rosenbaum went to a polygraph school a few years ago, and he insisted on doing the test. About five minutes into the test, he jumped in the boy's face, said we knew the kid was guilty and if he didn't speak up he'd get the needle for sure.

"That ended the polygraph and our hope to have him hypnotized. Svenson's since moved to Atlanta."

"Some people never change," I said with disgust. The two detectives glanced at each other and I realized the three of us had a common enemy in Rosenbaum.

"Do you think Svenson considered Cynthia Quinn more than a roommate?"

"We thought about it, but if he did, it was probably one-sided. Cynthia swung both ways, but she seemed to prefer women.

"Svenson knew her from church when they were kids. When she graduated from the University of Tennessee, she moved in with him to share rent. That's the take we got from several witnesses."

"So she was promiscuous."

"Even by today's standards, Lieutenant, she got around," Reagan said, taking off his rimless glasses. He wiped them with a treated lens tissue retrieved from a packet on the desk. A very fastidious man.

"So, Cynthia Quinn walked in her sleep, had nightmares, was promiscuous, paranoid about door locks and preferred women over men. You've just described an abused child — sexually or otherwise. That means she may have been sleeping with the kitchen knife. She may have started the violence rather than the perp having picked it up from the kitchen on his way in."

The two detectives locked eyes ever so briefly before Freed spoke in his contralto voice. "Lieutenant, it took us a while to arrive at that theory. We thought you never worked homicide."

"I didn't work homicide. But I saw a lot of them, listened to the investigators, *and* I write murder mysteries. It was a weak stomach, not a weak mind that kept me away from homicide. I had opportunities to play in the big league. I just didn't want to.

"So what's the deal on her adopted father — or, uncle, I suppose — Joshua Quinn?"

"Well, you've seen him on television, so you already know he's an asshole," Reagan said in his gravely voice. "But he was in Chattanooga that night at some kind of naval veteran's reunion. Hotel security where he was staying confirms that he didn't check out until ten the next morning.

"His wife, Emma, told us she had turned the phone off at home and taken a sedative, so they weren't notified officially until noon the next day.

"Phone records showed a call from his hotel to the victim's home phone at five-thirty the evening of the murder. He says they were planning a surprise birthday party for his wife. We didn't get to actually interview him for two days, but he had no visible injuries."

"Did you get DNA from him? He had plenty of time to come from Chattanooga after the five-thirty call and get back in time to check out of the hotel at nine the next morning."

"We asked, he became indignant, and we had no probable cause," Freed said. "We had him and his wife in for a conference and served refreshments, but he turned down anything that might have left DNA."

"All right, detectives, it sounds to me as if you've covered your bases. Why don't the two of you take a day off on the county?

"I'll dig into the files and I want both of you to focus on suspects you've talked to who set off alarm bells — even if they had good alibis. You've covered the obvious. In the morning, we'll start looking at the unlikely."

"Uh, Lieutenant, Chief Rosenbaum frowns on us leaving the building without checking with him first."

"While you're working for me, don't worry about Chief Rosenbaum. As long as I know where you are, that's good enough. Leave a card with your cell phone numbers, tell the dispatcher you're 10-6 until further notice and if Rosenbaum complains that you're *staying* busy, I'll deal with him."

"Aye, aye, Sir," Reagan said with a smile. Both of them left, looking a lot happier than they had when I arrived.

SIX

Kicked back in a recliner, I sipped coffee and looked out through the glass of the sun room we had added to the house four years ago. The dogwoods and redbuds were both in bloom and gave a festive atmosphere to the half acre backyard that had once been owned jointly by Jennifer and me before I moved out and gave her my half.

Some years in East Tennessee, it's still cool in early April; this year it's almost summer already. Nobody can predict the weather with much accuracy in the Tennessee Valley, which is surrounded by mountains on all sides.

A rabbit hopped furtively across the yard, pausing periodically to scan for dogs or other predators between nibbles. Coyotes have become prevalent in recent years, but generally move only at night, but terror is programmed into the genes of rabbits. That's why they're still around in an area that once teemed with panthers, bobcats, bears and red wolves.

"Mind if I join you?" I hadn't heard Jennifer come in.

"It's your house. There's fresh coffee in the carafe."

"How was your first day back at work?" She kicked off her shoes, sat down in a recliner that matched the one I was in, and poured herself a cup of black coffee. The business skirt slid back over her legs, revealing them to be as shapely as they had been twenty years ago, as she pushed herself back in the chair.

"Still trying to process it. I spent a few minutes doing the primate strut with my two detectives, but I think I came out okay. I gave them most of the day off – only partially to piss off Rosenbaum."

"That creep is still around? I'm surprised he hasn't permanently injured his career with the zipper on his pants."

"I heard that he's on his third wife, but he's slick when it comes to sucking up to whoever's in control. The previous sheriff could have solved the *Chief* Rosenbaum problem by firing *Sergeant* Rosenbaum fifteen years ago when he was accused of trying to force himself on a twenty-year-old."

"Is his current wife old enough to vote? Hmmmm... this coffee's good. Most of the time I just fix instant in the morning."

"I don't know how old she is. Why not just chew caffeine tablets?" I asked.

"We can't all be handy in the kitchen, Lieutenant."

Before I could respond, the new departmental cell phone I had been issued went off, startling me. I dug it out of my pants pocket. "This is Tempest."

"This is *Chief* Rosenbaum, *Lieutenant.* I don't like having two of my detectives disappear all afternoon. They're supposed to check out before they leave."

"They aren't *your* detectives, *Chief.* They're on special assignment and they are both veteran police officers, who don't need to be treated like children."

"I am still their supervisor --and yours-- and I expect to be updated every day on the progress of the investigation." I could envision his expression, eyes squinted and upper lip not moving at all.

"That's not going to happen, Timmy. You've been in charge of this investigation for two years, without progress. As I understand it, your only contribution so far was that you screwed up the polygraph exam and scared off the only eyewitness.

"If you've got a problem with the way I'm running this investigation, talk to the Sheriff. And don't bother me at home with nonsense." I closed the cell phone, ending the conversation.

"What was that all about?" Jennifer asked.

"That was Timmy Rosenbaum objecting to my style of personnel management."

"He used to at least keep it on the job," Jennifer said. "Maybe his obsessive compulsive disorder is getting worse."

"Maybe. Or maybe it's just his time of the month."

"How have you slept the last few nights?" Jennifer asked.

"I have been sleeping well, but it's time for me to make plans to move back home. The soreness is almost gone from the incision and obviously the device is working well."

"There's no need to get in a hurry — I've actually gotten used to eating breakfast again," Jennifer said with a laugh.

"Jen, we're getting to that comfortable stage again. We went through the hard part once already. Let's not reopen the wound."

Early the next morning I went by the Sheriff's office. As soon as I walked in, I knew Rosenbaum had already been by because of the way Sam was smiling.

"Timmy didn't waste any time did he?"

"His panties are in a big wad. I've already heard his side; now tell me what *really* happened," Sam said, grinning from ear to ear this time.

"He wants me to treat the detectives like little children the way he does. He *demanded* to be in on every step the investigation. The usual Rosenbaum nonsense."

"I take it you don't intend to keep him in the loop."

"No, I don't, Sam. As best I can tell, all he has done is impede the investigation. Why don't you just replace him? He's incompetent and everyone knows it."

"Shiloh, I've become one of those gutless politicians we both hate. I'll be running for office in a couple of years and Rosenbaum has clout. That's how he's survived all these years. Don't worry about him. I'll keep him out of your hair."

"That'll be easier said than done. But I'll take your word for it."

"Now that you've had time to look at the case and talk to the detectives, do you think I should let that national television show run with the case?"

"No, I don't. I think the case can be solved. I agree with the FBI profiler that the killer is local and he's not a serial killer. I *don't* think the description and composite is worth a damn, but I do believe he's local."

"What makes you think that composite's off?"

"I haven't talked to him yet, but I believe somebody scared the girl's roommate so badly that the composite is not worth anything. We just need to figure out why he's so scared."

Before Sam could say anything else, his secretary opened the door and said, "Sheriff, there's a Dr. John Olsen on the phone. What shall I tell him?"

"Tell him I'll call back. Well, Shiloh, I suppose you have work to do. I know I do."

"So Jennifer was telling the truth. *She* didn't discuss my case with the doctor --*you* did."

"John would *never* discuss a patient with anyone else. We just play golf together, Shiloh. I'm sure you'll agree that Dr. Olson is an ethical man."

He had me there, so I let it pass. "You're right, Sam. He's an ethical man and I do have work waiting."

Nonetheless, I thought about the situation all the way down to my office. *Ethical* can be a flexible, slippery word for cops. I wondered if it was any different for doctors. A man will do a lot that he wouldn't do otherwise when his friend's life is at stake. But I brought my attention back to the job at hand when I entered the office and found my two detectives already at work.

"Morning, Loo," Reagan said in his gravelly voice. "Can I get you a cup of joe?"

"Only if you're going to get coffee for yourself. I don't expect you to run errands for me." There was a decidedly cordial atmosphere this morning. *Loo* is a casual term for lieutenant that cops never use for a superior they don't like.

"I was just about to go get a cup, Loo. Detective Freed here don't drink coffee --he's a diet 7-Up man. When we're out in public, I make him drink his diet drink out of a coffee cup."

Reagan got up and moved his large frame ponderously out the door.

"You and Reagan seem to work well together," I said to Freed.

"Heck, yes. Reagan is a good man," Freed said. "We've narrowed the list you asked for, Loo, to three. Well, three that we *both* had a gut feeling about."

"In that case, we'll get started as soon as Reagan comes back."

Within five minutes, the big detective came back in with two cups of coffee. I saw that he had already prepared it, black with sugar, the way he had seen me fix it the day before.

"Gentlemen, proceed," I said.

"We both feel strongly about the uncle — or the adopted father, as he prefers to be called — not just because he's an asshole," Reagan said in his deep, gravelly voice, "though he is. A witness from the drugstore where Cynthia traded had her arguing with an older man who matched the description of her adopted father, just a few days before the murder."

"There was a security video, but it was such a low quality, even with enhancement, all we can really tell is that he was husky, around six feet and has a full head of dark hair. One of the clerks remembered the argument and put his age at fifty, but she was twenty herself, so the age could be thirty to sixty — which could be any one of thousands of men in this county.

"We were looking at Joshua Quinn very closely until his alibi about being in Chattanooga checked out. Both of us had a gut feeling, but we couldn't break the alibi. We couldn't prove that he *didn't* leave, but there's no doubt he was there — at least he was checked in during that time."

"The city of Knoxville has cameras at most major intersections these days," I said. "We need to contact the police department about the tickets issued that night. It probably won't help but we don't have anything to lose."

Freed nodded and made a note on a large yellow pad he was holding.

"The next suspect that we both felt strongly about was an ex-convict named Jimmy West. He lived in the apartment complex and had asked Cynthia out on several occasions. She finally dressed him down in front of neighbors and told him she wouldn't go out with him under *any* circumstances. The neighbors said he was pretty well steamed at her.

"He has a long rap sheet, everything from petty theft to drug trafficking. His alibi is an outlaw biker named David Winslow. We brought Winslow in and leaned on him hard, but he left here insisting that West was there from four in the evening until well after midnight. Winslow is the bouncer and doorman at the Ruby Club."

"The Ruby Club, a strip bar on 25W, right?"

"That's the place, Loo. A real shit-hole," Reagan said.

"Cynthia's roommate is the third suspect we both had a gut feeling about," Reagan continued. "We don't think he did it, but we think he knows a lot more than he's telling us. Maybe a ménage à trois gone bad. "

"Is there any possibility of getting the roommate back up here to talk to us again?"

"No, Loo, he's pretty firmly established in Atlanta. Thanks to Chief Stiffy, our best witness and one of the chief suspects is 200 miles away. His mother has tried to talk to him, but after Chief Stiffy finished with him on the polygraph, he never spoke to us again."

I decided to let the reference to Rosenbaum as "Chief Stiffy" go by. Technically it's bad management, but strategically it was to my benefit. Besides, I'd called him a lot worse.

"Here's our opening game plan, detectives. After we have lunch, I'm going out to re-interview that biker and you two are going to see our witness's mother again.

"The two of you are going to hint around that we might be able to put the killer away and clear her son, *if* he'll come back and talk to us again. If the boy is keeping quiet because he's afraid of the murderer, the idea of seeing the murderer locked away might do the trick. Of course, if he's involved, we will *have* to go to him.

"Now where would you gentlemen like to eat today?"

"Well," Freed almost warbled, "there's a Mexican restaurant on Merchant Drive that feeds officers at half-price."

"Does the Regas feed officers at half price?" I asked.

"The High Sheriff, maybe." Reagan chuckled.

"Fortunately, I have a credit card from the department, so we don't *need* the half-price. Let's go to Regas for lunch."

"Golly, you won't get any argument from us on that, Loo. We *never* look a gift horse in the mouth." Freed said.

It was like icing on the cake when Chief Rosenbaum came in to the Regas while we were there. He was with an attractive blonde that I recognized as a television reporter. He didn't speak, but I knew that seeing us there ruined his meal.

The Ruby Club is a dump of a strip joint. It isn't as bad as some, but the expensive clubs are in West Knoxville where the money is. I knocked on a large red door with an ornate façade, and it was opened quickly by a large man of forty or so with a big belly, a full bushy beard of a reddish color, and hair pulled back in a ponytail.

"Cover charge is 10 bucks," he said gruffly.

"Are you David Winslow?"

"Who wants to know?" he said, sounding even less cordial.

I held up my badge case. "Lieutenant Shiloh Tempest, Sheriff's Department."

"Come on in. I hope this ain't going to take long. I'm busy. The three o'clock rush will be starting any minute now."

We stepped into the large, darkened room and I saw that things had not changed since I was a patrol officer. A couple of bored-looking dancers stood at the bar sipping drinks and the bartender, dressed in a tuxedo shirt and tie, looked at me with a question his eyes.

"What do you want to drink, lieutenant? I stay clean these days – while *I'm* on duty."

"You need to improve your attitude, Winslow, or the first thing we'll talk about is that you're a convicted felon and as such are not supposed to work where alcoholic beverages are sold. This dump could lose its license."

"I didn't mean to be rude, lieutenant. Let's sit down at a table. Can I get you something to drink? A coke or juice?" Winslow knew how to play the game *suck to the bulls* as bikers say, when he had to.

"That's better," I said, taking a seat at one of the tables, from which I could see the door and everyone in the room at the same time. "No thanks on the drink.

"Two years ago, you told detectives from the sheriff's department that Jimmy West was here while a murder in which he was a suspect took place. I would like for you reconsider that statement. I don't think West was here at all that night."

"That was a long time ago, Lieutenant. I just have to assume that what I said that night was true." He shifted uneasily in his seat, then glanced away.

"No, Mr. Winslow, that wasn't such a long time ago. In fact, I think you remember it like it was yesterday. Here's why. If Jimmy West were a brother, you would lie to protect him, no matter what I threatened to do. But he *isn't* a brother.

"That tells me that West paid you to give him an alibi — probably in drugs, since that's what he does for a living. I don't care about the drugs, and so far you haven't lied under oath. With these thoughts in mind, I ask you to reconsider what you remember. If you *should* remember that West really wasn't here that night because he *really* wasn't, we'll both be okay.

"On the other hand, if you lie to me — and I'll find out if you're lying — I'm going to call a cruiser and haul your smelly ass to jail. After a little while, I'll release you without charges. Then I'll call your clubhouse and tell Cletus to thank you for the information."

"How do you know Cletus?"

"I worked criminal intelligence for five years. I still owe Cletus a few favors and he owes me a couple. We've never *liked* each other, but I've always been truthful with him. So you need to decide if you want Jimmy West's good will or *my* good will."

"Cletus wouldn't believe an outsider over a brother," Winslow said, his nervousness showing through.

"Maybe not right away, but the *suspicion* would always be there. Are you really willing to go through that much trouble for a drug dealing scumbag like Jimmy West?"

"All right, West was *not* here that night – not that I remember. Are the two of us okay?"

"Are you telling me the truth this time?"

"Yeah, I probably would've said he was here just because a cop asked me, even if West hadn't made it worth my while. You know how it is? But he ain't worth a lot of trouble to me," the big biker said.

"I really appreciate that, Mr. Winslow."

As I pushed my chair back to get to get up, I saw Winslow glance at the door and smile to himself. "Lieutenant Tempest, you must have some kind of magic powers. Jimmy West just walked in."

My first impulse was the correct one. I almost left without looking in West's direction and went outside to call for backup. Unfortunately, I seldom follow the correct impulse. I stood and turned, then locked eyes with Jimmy West. *The wicked flee when no man pursues*, it says in the Bible. He had no idea who I was, but he bolted for the door. And I ran after him.

West was a medium sized man, taller than I, but not nearly as heavy. I grabbed him by the collar and jerked him back as he was trying to insert his key in the door of a classic yellow Corvette, then slung him away from it. He threw a punch; I grabbed his arm, twisted it behind his back. "Give it up, West!"

As I spoke, he pushed backwards, slamming me into the Corvette, and his elbow drove into my midsection, directly on top of my brand-new pacemaker incision. I yelled in pain, then blacked out for a few seconds. When I opened my eyes again, the Corvette was throwing gravel behind it as it fishtailed across the parking lot.

Gasping into my portable radio, I gave a description of West and the Corvette. Then I spoke into the portable radio very distinctly: "Have a cruiser meet me at the produce market just north of the Ruby Club."

I climbed into the little blue Chevrolet compact I had been given to drive, with pain radiating from the center of my chest, seemingly to all points of my body, and drove the short distance to the produce market.

I got out and leaned against the car trying not to breathe too deeply. It was probably only three or four minutes, but it seemed like an hour before a patrol car pulled up and a concerned-looking young patrol officer with a shaved head got out.

"Are you all right, Lieutenant?" He asked.

"No, I'm *not* all right. I just had a defibrillator put in and I pulled something loose in the scuffle with West. I didn't want to go down in front of a crowd at that lowlife bar. I need you to secure my gear and call an ambulance. I guess you'd better tell them to hurry."

That was the last thing I remembered until I woke up in the hospital.

SEVEN

My escapade at the Ruby Club had involved all three of the basic plots of fiction: an individual at war with himself; an individual at war with the forces of nature; and an individual at war with another individual. That thought was on my mind before I opened my eyes; plus the realization of how incredibly stupid my actions had been.

"Hoss, I brought you back to run a case, not fight with thugs half your age. Do I need to assign you a bodyguard or will you give me your word to behave yourself in a manner befitting a man of your age and physical condition?"

Sheriff Sam Renfro was sitting by my hospital bed when I opened my eyes. He was in a rumpled pale-gray suit with his maroon silk tie loosened. He was in need of a shave and almost looked his age, which was somewhere around fifty.

"Am I dying? That's the only reason I can think of why the High Sheriff would be sitting by my bed?"

"No, Hoss, you ain't going to die. But if I understood John Olsen, you pulled loose one of the leads to your heart during the scuffle and they had to fix it. I just hung around so Jennifer wouldn't be by herself. God knows the poor woman has put up with enough heartache for twenty years. She went down for coffee and a sandwich."

"What time is it, Sam?"

"It's a little after four in the morning. You were out for a little over six hours after the surgery." Sam stood up and stretched. "There's a BOLO out for Jimmy West. It's just a matter of time until we find him.

"Oh yeah, and your detectives were here until midnight. You seem to inspire a lot of loyalty to have only been their boss for a couple of days. I sent them home, but that redheaded Freed boy with the squeaky voice was almost dancing from foot to foot. He had something to tell you. They should be back around nine o'clock this morning."

"They just like me because I took them to Regas for lunch and Rosenbaum came in and couldn't do anything about them taking over an hour for lunch. I don't suppose Chief Stiffy has been in to check on me?"

"No, the Chief has not been in. Try not to let it get you down. If it's okay with you, I'm heading home."

"Sam, you're good friend."

"Don't go maudlin on me, Hoss. I'll see you in a couple of days."

Sam left, and Jennifer came back about five minutes later. Apparently she had freshened up because every hair was in place and her makeup --what little she wears-- was flawless.

"Well, Tempest, did you get it out of your system or do we have events like this to look forward to in the future?"

"He sucker punched me," I said.

"You mean he punched a sucker. Honestly, Tempest. You're not up to street fights. Why didn't you just call patrol?"

"I'm like an old Beagle, Jen. The rabbit ran and I chased it."

"Well, at least we don't have to go to the trouble of rounding up your stuff this time. It's already at the house. At least, I *presume* you'll have the good sense to stay a few days longer."

"Yes, Jen. I appreciate the invitation." I saw that my choice of words had hurt her by the expression that passed over her face, but she didn't say anything about it.

"All right, then. I'm going home. I have a case in federal court at nine. I'll see you later. She leaned over and kissed me on the cheek. I wanted more than anything to put my arms around her at that moment and hold her close like the old days — but I didn't.

After Jen left, a chubby little nurse with a bad bleach job came in and put a shot of morphine into my IV and I drifted away.

"Say *something*," Freed's wavering voice penetrated my drug-induced slumber. "He looks like he's waking up."

"Naw, let him sleep," Reagan's gravelly voice was more of a roar than a whisper.

"I'm awake, guys. The Sheriff said you two were here last night. I appreciate that. You have new info, Freed?"

"Yeah, Loo." The redheaded detective appeared ready to burst. "A Cadillac SUV registered to Joshua Quinn was caught on camera running a red light on Kingston Pike at 20:17 hours, the night Cynthia Quinn was murdered. The fine was paid with a check from his wife."

I smiled. "Good work. What about Robert Svenson's mother?"

"She says she'll try to convince him to come back and talk to us again," Reagan said. "Loo, there's something else you ought to know. Chief Rosenbaum came to the office right after you were hurt yesterday, while we were getting ready to come over here. He demanded to know what else we had uncovered in the case."

"What did you tell him?"

"We didn't tell him diddly-squat!" Freed answered.

"Good. Here's what I want you to do today. Have a new filing cabinet moved to our office. Throw in some suspect files that we aren't using and get a new padlock. The two of you keep current duplicate case files, but keep them with you in your briefcases. If Rosenbaum is overcome by curiosity, he'll go for the new padlock," I said.

"You know, Rosenbaum has hated my guts since we worked patrol together, and nobody likes having a case they've been working from day one pulled from under them, but he's being more obstructionist about this case than I've ever seen from him before."

"Loo, Chief Stiffy wasn't on this case from day one. He was on vacation — fishing in Florida — for the first week," Freed said.

"Rosenbaum was fishing in Florida? He usually spends his vacations attending seminars or tech schools."

"Yeah, he was fishing all right," Reagan said. "He has a newspaper article on his bulletin board with his picture on the front page of the local paper. He got bit by a small shark or a barracuda while he was there and had to be stitched up at a local hospital. You know what a publicity whore he is.

"If a shark or barracuda bit Timmy, so much for professional courtesy," I said.

"As soon as he got back, he started personally supervising the case," Freed said, trying unsuccessfully to stifle a chuckle at my comment. "That was how he ended up being the polygraph operator that day. At first he hounded us for daily updates, but by the time you took over, he was down to about a once-a-week inquiry."

"You'd think a barracuda or a shark *would* have given Rosenbaum a little professional courtesy," Reagan said, setting off Freed into a laughing fit.

EIGHT

By the third day after my most recent surgery, I felt well enough to go back to work. Jen complained that I needed more rest, but I'm not a man who ever learned to relax, let alone *rest*. It's like I was born in a state of excitement.

After parking in the basement of the City- County building, I took the elevator up to the mezzanine and walked to the elevators in the center of the building. As I was getting on the elevator, I met Tim Rosenbaum. "Chief," I said with a nod.

His lips tightened and his nose flared. "Lieutenant. You're looking well for a man who damaged his pacemaker four days ago."

"It was a defibrillator, not a pacemaker. I mend very quickly, Chief." The elevator came to a stop and Rosenbaum stepped off ahead of me and walked away rapidly. His Prussian-like, upright stride reminded me of something an old patrol officer had said about Rosenbaum when he was still a rookie: "That boy walks like he has a police baton up his ass."

The sheriff was not in his office, so I left a message with the secretary that I was back at work. I went back to the elevator and rode down two levels to the area where the criminal investigation division is located. I scanned my ID card across the sensor and walked back to the little office I shared with Freed and Reagan.

The smell of fresh-brewed coffee tickled my nostrils as I entered. I saw that a coffee pot had been installed on the table behind Reagan's desk. There was a carryout bag from Burger King on Freed's desk.

"Morning, Loo. Welcome back. I decided since there are two of us drinking coffee now, I'd set up our own pot. Freed brought in some sausage and biscuits. We didn't know if it was on your diet or not, but we like them," Reagan said.

"I like sausage and biscuits too. Let me pick up half the cost of the coffee pot, since the two of us will be using it."

"Naw, I got it from down in the evidence room, Loo." He poured me a cup of coffee, put in a teaspoon of sugar and handed it to me.

"Thanks, Reagan — and thanks for the biscuits, Freed." I reached into the bag, took out a sausage and biscuit, unwrapped it and took a large bite. I took a seat at my desk, leaned back and took a sip coffee. "Cop soul food and an interesting case. It doesn't get much better than this."

"You got that, Loo. My arteries may be clogging, but I sure do enjoy my sausage and biscuits." Freed said.

"Any word from Svenson's mother while I was off."

"Yeah, he told his mother he ain't coming back to talk to us," Freed said.

"I guess we can't blame him," I said. "If he is innocent, the incident with the polygraph probably left a bad taste in his mouth — if he's guilty, he's got two hundred miles between him and the law."

"Are we going to bring Joshua Quinn down here and talk to him about the ticket that was issued to his Lincoln while he was supposed to be in Chattanooga?" Reagan asked, consuming half of a sausage and biscuit with one bite.

"I don't think so. We don't know whether he was driving the Cadillac Escalade on the trip to Chattanooga. If we try to talk to Quinn or his wife — who was supposed to be sick in bed — I am afraid they'll lawyer up. I'm going to have the Sheriff set up a new meeting with the two of them for another shot at DNA.

"Meanwhile, I want the two of you to drive down to Chattanooga and check into the hotel where he was staying. Spend the evening and tomorrow morning talking to staff. Stay over another day, if you need to.

"Go to finance and get a couple hundred dollars cash to spread around if that's what it takes to jog some memories, and pick up a credit card. Just make sure you keep your cell phones on. Put your meals on the credit card."

The two detectives looked at each other and smiled. Reagan said: "Loo, we like your management style."

"If you mean treating grown men like grown men, it's the way I've always done it. By the way, now that we've got the dogs-sniffing-asses thing out of the way, you can call me by my first name or my last."

"Loo, if it's all the same to you, it's been a long time since we've had a supervisor we've *respected* enough to call by his rank." Reagan said.

"Suit yourselves. Have a good trip and stay out of trouble."

When they were gone, I called the Sheriff's secretary. "Madeline, this is Shiloh Tempest. Will you see if the Sheriff has time to talk to me?" I waited for about thirty seconds before she came back with an affirmative answer. "Thanks, Madeline. I'll be up in a couple minutes."

Outside the Sheriff's door, Madeline smiled and waved me through. She had been with the previous sheriff a dozen years and Sam had kept her on. Unlike previous administrations, there had been no bloodbath when Sam assumed office.

As I entered, Sam hung up the telephone. "How's the bionic man today? I hope you haven't tried to leap over any tall buildings or stop any bullets."

"No, but I just sent Freed and Reagan to Chattanooga to follow up on a lead. A Cadillac Escalade belonging to Joshua Quinn was caught on camera, running a red light on Kingston Pike, just a short distance from where Cynthia was murdered while he was supposed to be in Chattanooga."

"Can you put him inside the car?" Sam asked.

"That's what my two detectives are going to try to do the next two days. I don't want to cause him to lawyer up by asking questions now. In fact, I'd like to have you invite him and his wife in to introduce yourself and me to them. If you'll serve light refreshments, I'll see if we can get a DNA sample from him. It was tried once before, but I'd like to take another shot at it."

"Sure, I can do that. I need to do it as a PR thing, anyway..."

Sam was interrupted as his secretary opened the door. "Sheriff, Chief Rosenbaum is on the phone *demanding* to speak to you. What shall I tell him?"

"Put him on line four." Sam turned as she closed the door and said, "My predecessor took out the intercom system because he didn't like it. I'm waiting for the equipment to put it back. Excuse me for just a moment." He picked up the phone, pushed the button marked *4* and spoke: "This is the Sheriff. How can I help you, Chief?"

Sam listen briefly. "I'm aware of that, Chief. Lieutenant Tempest has already filled me in on it. And they're not *your* detectives — they're all *my* detectives. I have approved the trip and I would suggest that you stop obstructing the two of them. Are we clear, Chief?" Sam hung up the phone.

"Sorry about that, Shiloh. I'll have Madeline set up a meeting with the Quinns. Keep me updated, if you will. If you'll excuse me, I have to meet with that windbag who passes himself off as the mayor of this county."

When Jennifer came in, I was sitting in the recliner in the sunroom with my wireless laptop. "How was your day?" She asked.

"Did you know that Volusia County, Florida is the shark bite capital of the United States?" I asked.

"Volusia County? That's where Daytona Beach is, right?"

"Daytona Beach, Daytona Shores, New Smyrna Beach and several others. Bull sharks spawn in the lagoons."

"Any particular reason why you're reading about sharks?"

"My detectives told me that Tim Rosenbaum was attacked by a shark a couple of years ago at Daytona Beach. Well, actually they said a shark or a barracuda, but I looked it up on the Internet. The newspaper article from Daytona says he was fishing in the surf when he dropped his pocket knife and when he reached into the water to get it, a shark grabbed his hand"

"You would think that sharks would show Rosenbaum a little professional courtesy," Jennifer said, taking off the wine colored jacket she had worn over an ivory silk blouse.

I smiled. "That's exactly what I said to the detectives – who agreed."

"No coffee today?" Jen asked.

"Actually, I made some about a half-hour ago, and then forgot about it. I'll go get it."

"Just sit still. You made it; the least I can do is carry it in here."

Jennifer came back a few minutes later and I saw she had ditched her shoes. It's almost always the first thing she does upon entering the house. She put down the tray, poured coffee for both of us and handed me two tickets.

"So Steve Earle's coming to the Tennessee Theatre again? It's been a while since I've seen him perform."

"One of my clients gave them to me as partial payment. He'll be spending the next four years as a resident of a government facility."

"Would this be the client with two kilos of junk? If it is, he must have really given them a big fish to walk with four years."

"You know I can't discuss the confidential details of a client. But I'm hoping to get as good a deal for Josie Fletcher. I'm afraid I won't — she has no drug lords to trade for leniency."

"Fletcher... is she the woman who stabbed her husband to death with the knife she was using to slice his birthday cake? In front of twenty witnesses."

"That's the *gist* of it," Jennifer said, "but there were *twelve* years of constant abuse leading up to the moment when she finally had enough. She bought a *yellow* cake, for God's sake, instead of chocolate! He was whispering to her what he was going to do after everyone left, because of the wrong kind of cake."

I started to make a flip comment about incompetent murderers and bad timing, but something in her expression made me hold back. Jennifer had been an abused child *and* an abused wife before I met her. The case had to be affecting her at a deep personal level.

"So, are you up to the Steve Earle concert tomorrow night?" Jennifer asked, pushing herself back into the recliner and changing the subject.

"Why not?" I said. Before I heard Steve Earle's song *John Walker's Blues*, I hadn't been to a concert since Lou Christie had come to Knoxville with Mitch Ryder and the Detroit Wheels as the opening act in 1966 or thereabouts.

NINE

A surprise visitor came to my office on Monday morning. It was Chief Tim Rosenbaum. "Do you have a minute?" he asked.

"Sure," I said. "Pull up a chair and sit down. I would offer coffee, but I haven't made any. I got here early today to go over some paperwork. But I forgot, you don't drink coffee, anyway. You were healthy before it was fashionable."

"We have gotten off to a bad start this time around. I'd like to mend some fences. We go back a long way, Shiloh."

"We first got off to the wrong start almost three decades ago, Chief. What's different about now?"

"We were both kids then. There's no reason why we can't work together as adults now," he said. "At least that's how I feel about it."

"That sounds fair enough, Chief."

"So, how was your weekend?" he asked.

"Jennifer and I went to a Steve Earle concert at the Tennessee Theatre," I said.

"Is this Steve Earle a new singer?"

"No, he's sort of like Warren Zevon, who died not long ago. They'd both been around awhile but I didn't discover either of them until a few years ago."

He nodded his head and I saw that he didn't know who Warren Zevon was either, but I decided to let it go. "How was your weekend, Chief?"

"Call me *Tim*. We've known each other long enough for first names," he said. "My wife and I drove down to Nashville for the Grand Ole Opry."

"Is your wife the woman I saw you with at Regas last week?"

"No," he flushed just a little, "that was a reporter and we were on business."

"Are you doing much fishing lately?" I asked.

"Why do you ask?"

"I was doing some research on sharks a while back and ran across a story in a Florida newspaper that said you were the victim of a shark attack. I just wondered if you were still fishing."

"You saw it on the *Internet?*" I had no doubt he would be on the computer five minutes after he left my office. His name in print had always been like an aphrodisiac to him.

"No, it was a pretty bad experience. I was standing in the surf fishing and dropped my pocket knife. But you already know that since you read the article."

"It was a hell of a way to find out you don't really like to fish," I said. "Did it do much damage?"

"No," he held his right palm up and there was a thin scar. "It was a jagged bite, but the doctor who stitched it straightened it out. It was a small shark that mistook my hand for a fish. Most of the Volusia County bites are minor."

We sat quietly for a few minutes, having exhausted our social niceties. Finally, he asked what he had come to ask: "How is the case coming?"

"Well, I only got the case a week ago, so I guess it's going well."

"I suppose Reagan and Freed are back from Chattanooga by now," he said, fishing for information.

"I suppose so, Tim. I told them to stay as long as necessary. I'll know if they're back here in a few minutes. If they don't come in, they are still in Chattanooga."

"You have a low key management style. I try to keep track of my detectives."

"My style is to treat adults like adults," I said.

He let the dig pass. "Anything I might be interested in?"

"I don't know what might be of interest to you, Tim. And like I said, I haven't talked to my two detectives yet about what they found in Chattanooga."

"Would you mind if I sat in when you debrief them this morning, Shiloh?"

"Yes, I *would* mind, Tim. This is my case now and I play my cards close to my vest. Need to know basis. But you already know that."

"I'm trying to be *reasonable*, Shiloh! Those two detectives are under my supervision, and you're only here temporarily." Rosenbaum's face had turned two shades darker. He was never one who liked being told he couldn't have something he wanted.

"Did you really think it was going to be that easy? Did you think you could waltz in here and play me like a like cheap kazoo?"

He stood up suddenly, turned and walked to the door, and almost ran into Freed and Reagan as they were entering. He brushed by them without acknowledging their presence.

"Excuse us, Chief," Reagan said over his shoulder. Seeing me, the big detective asked: "What got up *his* ass?"

"My *foot* was up his ass." I stood up, went to the little table behind Reagan's desk and began to make coffee, without further comment.

"Loo, I can make the coffee," Reagan said.

"Detective Reagan, we both drink the coffee. I can make it as well as you. In fact, it would've been done already, but Chief Rosenbaum came in and tried to work me like a suspect. He wanted to sit in on our meeting this morning and I told him no. That's why he left in such a rage as you were coming in."

"Loo, this morning I brought in pork tenderloin and biscuits with egg and cheese and a side of tater tots," Freed said. I didn't even have to look to know that the two detectives were looking at each other meaningfully.

"Freed, that takeout could get expensive. Let me chip in."

"Don't worry about it, Lieutenant," Freed said. "I used the last of the bribe money to pay for the biscuits."

"Did we get our money's worth from the bribe money?"

"We sure did, Loo. We still don't know if Joshua Quinn was driving the Escalade, but we did learn a few things about him," Reagan said.

"Give me a biscuit, Freed, and tell me all about Joshua Quinn."

"Loo, I bought everybody *two* biscuits this morning, so you can eat one now and have one with your coffee."

"Freed, you sure do eat a lot for a skinny redheaded guy." I said.

"That he does," Reagan said. "If I ate the way he does, I'd weigh four hundred pounds, instead of two-sixty."

I took the wrapper off my biscuit and pork tenderloin and bit into it. "Tell me Joshua's secrets."

"He drinks too much and gets rowdy," Freed said. "We talked to the chief of security at the Marriott and his officers had to break up an altercation Quinn had with one of his old shipmates while he was there."

"That's interesting to know," I said, savoring the taste and texture of biscuit, cheese, egg and pork tenderloin, knowing that my cardiologist and friend John Olsen would be aghast to see me enjoying hillbilly soul food.

"Gets better," Reagan cut in. "It cost half the bribe money, but a helpful bellhop told us that he hooked Quinn up with a prostitute Thursday night. It was so expensive because we got him to point the girl out.

"We found her working the bar and flashed our shields. She was so relieved that we weren't the local police, she really opened up. Quinn paid extra for a little role-playing. Want to guess what the role-playing was about?"

"Daddy and his little girl?"

"*Bingo*, Loo." Reagan said. "He has a game about getting it on with his *imaginary* daughter, and within twenty-four hours, his *adopted* daughter is murdered in her own bedroom.

"But we still can't put him in the Caddy that night. If he was driving it, he either didn't buy gas or he paid cash. But Chattanooga's less than an hour away. He could have made easily made two trips without filling up, even in a gas guzzler.

"Loo, Freed and I think it's time to pull in his wife and sweat her. She might give him up if it looks like she's going down with him — or she knew about the prostitute."

"You guys did some good police work," I said. "But I still want a shot at getting DNA from Quinn before we risk having him lawyer up on us. The Sheriff is arranging another meeting with refreshments."

"It's your call, Loo." Reagan said. "And it looks like our coffee's done." He got up and opened his briefcase. He rummaged around, then held up two white mugs that read *Thou shalt not kill* on one side, and on the other *Homicide: We Work for God.*

"Very nice, Reagan. When did you get them?" I asked.

"I've had them a while, Loo. Ordered them on the Internet. But until the last few days, I felt like I'd lost the right to use them. I put our names on the bottom."

I didn't know what to say, so I didn't say anything as he filled the cups and handed me mine — black with one sugar.

"Lieutenant, I made up a dummy file and put a padlock on the filing case like you said. We'll have the only keys," Freed said with a big smile. "If Chief Stiffy gets in, he'll have to pry it open." The redheaded detective was like a kid, easily pleased.

The office phone rang as I was taking my first sip of coffee. Freed answered the phone with a cheerful, "Homicide Taskforce, Detective Freed."

He listened quietly for a moment and his mobile face lit up. "Hold on, I'll tell my lieutenant." He put his hand over the mouthpiece. "Loo, patrol stopped Jimmy West an hour ago for driving on an expired tag, and served the warrants on him for his assault on you. You want him in the interrogation room?"

"You bet your ass we do."

West sat nervously in the interrogation room as we watched him through the one-way mirror. I had seen West's picture and met him briefly during our scuffle, but up close it was obvious that he wasn't just a drug dealer, but also a consumer. He was wearing a leather jacket in spite of the warm weather, and could truly be called cadaverous. His teeth all appeared to be rotting — a sign of meth use — and he was jumpy.

"You want the first shot, Loo?" Reagan asked.

"No, I think you two should do it. You need to explain how he nearly killed your beloved lieutenant and how upset you are."

Both detectives suddenly had big smiles on their faces. "We read you loud and clear, Loo." Reagan said.

Watching from the other side of the glass, I saw West look up as they entered the bare room with green walls where he sat cuffed to a metal table bolted to the floor. Reagan, whose sheer size made him look formidable, even with the empty shoulder holster, sat down directly across from him and the thin, wiry Freed stood to West's left, arms crossed.

They both stared at him without speaking until he began to squirm in his chair. "I been here before," West said. "You can't scare me by starin' at me. You try to lean on me and I'll call my lawyer. All you got on me is assault and fleein' to avoid arrest."

The two detectives continued to stare.

"Did you hear me? I ain't no cherry. I know my rights."

"Detective Freed, did you hear that? This little weasel knows his rights. I wonder if he knows there's nobody else here except him and the two cops whose lieutenant he almost killed?"

"Let's ask him," Freed said, leaning towards West. "Did you know you almost killed the man who trained both of us — a man we love like a brother?"

"I didn't *mean* to hurt him. All I did was hit him with my elbow so I could get away. I ain't a violent man. Look at my rap sheet."

"Lieutenant Tempest had just had a defibrillator put in," Reagan said. "You jerked the wires loose when you elbowed him — something you just confessed to, by the way — and he still ain't out of the woods yet."

"There ain't no cops with bad hearts," West said. But they had his attention.

"Did you hear that, Detective Freed? Now this piece of human excrement is calling me a liar. West, we got cops with wooden legs, glass eyes and all kinds of false parts. You hit our lieutenant in the chest and tore his new defibrillator loose. If he dies, the charge becomes felony murder!"

"I think I need a lawyer," West said.

"Well, you can have a lawyer, West. But the minute you lawyer up, any chance of making a deal is down the toilet," Freed said.

"What kind of deal?" Suddenly there was hope on his rodent-like face.

"Well, it just happens there's a case we want to close the books on more than we want to punish you for hurting our lieutenant," Reagan said.

"I told you two years ago I had nothin' to do with killin' Cynthia Quinn. I *liked* her. Besides," West said. "I was at the Ruby Club when it happened and I got an alibi."

"You *had* an alibi. But the truth is, we don't think you killed the girl, anyway — we think it was the roommate, Svenson — and we think you may have seen something that night."

The carrot and the stick was probably used by Roman cops in the first century. If West admitted that he wasn't at the Ruby Club that night, he would have opened the door the two detectives wanted to enter.

"Naw, I ain't fallin' for that. David Winslow is my alibi."

Reagan snorted contemptuously. "Did you hear that, Freed? He ain't figured it out yet and he *saw* the lieutenant talking to Winslow. He fingered you, West. Winslow didn't stay bought."

"Yeah, genius." Freed put his lips close to West's ear. "If you don't get with the program, you're going to end up with a needle in your arm for Cynthia Quinn's murder and maybe for what you did to our lieutenant."

Before the flustered West could respond, I opened the door. "What's going on here? I told the two of you to wait until I arrived before you questioned him."

"Lieutenant, we thought..." Reagan began.

"I know what you thought. When are you two going to learn we don't work people over with rubber hoses any more? Get out!

"In fact, go get us some coffee. How do you drink your coffee, Mister West?" I asked.

"I drink it black, Lieutenant," he stammered.

"What are you two thugs waiting on?"

"Nothing, Loo," Freed said. "We're on our way out for coffee."

When the door closed, I looked at West and shook my head. "I'm sorry about this, Mister West. I can't watch them every moment. They're still upset about our little accident the other night."

"They said you might die because you'd just had a pacemaker put in."

"That's true," I said, opening my shirt. "Here's the new incision. They haven't been able to get the rhythm back since you accidentally hit me in the chest."

"I... I'm sorry about that," he said. His eyes opened wide as he looked at the fresh stitches.

"I'll make a note of your remorse — just in case worse comes to worse and you do end up on trial for felony murder. *I* know you didn't do it on purpose. I wish I could get you out of their reach, but unless you're willing to tell them where you *really* were that night, you'll be here awhile."

"Suppose I admitted I was somewhere else besides the apartment complex and could prove it --would they let me off the hook for accidentally hurtin' you?"

"I think so. They really want to close the Quinn case. And I'd be willing to talk to the district attorney on your behalf."

"I'd just hate to be in your shoes if this pacemaker stops working. You might or might not get to trial. Cops are unreasonable when it comes to one of their own. Accidents happen. Prisoners try to escape." I stopped and let it sink in.

"Lieutenant, suppose I was in another state, say doin' a crime a lot less serious than murder — how long would it take to get me extradited?"

"If it's a serious case, detectives from whatever jurisdiction you're talking about would just come and get you. If you didn't fight it, you could possibly be out of here tomorrow."

"In that case, I have a statement to make."

"Go ahead, but first I need you to sign a release that you were read your Miranda warning." I opened a drawer on my side of the table and removed a standard release and a yellow legal pad.

He signed the release. "You want me to tell you before I write it down?"

"However you want to do it, Mister West."

"Let me tell you first. I'll need help with the spelling."

"All right," I replied. "Let's hear it."

"Me and another guy," West leaned forward in a conspiratorial manner, "was robbin' a drug store in Hickory, North Carolina, the night Cynthia was killed."

"You mean, as in an *armed robbery*?"

"God, no! I wouldn't cop to armed robbery so easy. We broke in and stole a shitload of painkillers."

"Who was the other guy?"

"Do I *have* to give him up?"

"Yes. Besides, you can use him as a chip to get less time."

"His name is Chandler Watson. He lives in Hickory. He came to me with the plan because he'd never done a burglary before."

The door to the interrogation room opened. "Loo, we got your coffee," Freed said.

"You two come on in. Mister West has confessed to a burglary the night Cynthia was killed. You'll need to get the details and call the Hickory, North

Carolina, detectives so they can verify it and then come and pick up Mister West. You're to treat him like a gentleman until that time. Are we clear on that?"

They both nodded, faces emotionless, but West had something else to say to me.

"Lieutenant, I'm sorry I hurt you. And I want to thank you for everything you've done for me today."

I nodded and managed to keep a straight face.

TEN

Jennifer was already sitting in the sunroom when I arrived that evening, going over some kind of document on the little writing table at the back.

"You're home early," I said, taking off my tweed jacket with leather sleeve patches that had gone in and out of style twice since I bought it. I saw that she had carried in a carafe of coffee on a tray. I put in one lump, then slowly filled the cup so I wouldn't have to stir it. Economy of motion.

"I'm going over Josie Fletcher's case, trying to find a way to make a jury see what she endured for twelve years. The prosecutor won't budge an inch on the second degree murder charge. It's going to be a travesty of justice if she gets the maximum. At the very most, what she did was voluntary manslaughter."

"Was there a police history of domestic disturbance or trips to the emergency room?" I asked.

"Two trips to the emergency room over twelve years. He was clever — openhanded slaps, shoving and dragging her around by her hair — and she was the perfect Southern housewife, enduring stoically," Jennifer said.

"Did you consider temporary insanity?"

"Of course I did. Josie wouldn't cooperate, though. I think she still halfway believes it was her fault."

"If your client won't cooperate, all you can do is work with what you have."

"I suppose so. How was your day?" She paused and took a sip of coffee.

"Very productive. I'm thinking about taking a trip to Atlanta, maybe for a day or two. Would you like to go down and do some shopping?"

"I think I can get away. I've pretty much put everything aside except Josie's case until it goes to trial and that's almost a week away. Why are you going to Atlanta?"

"To interview a witness, if he'll talk to me."

"Count me in," she said.

"Well, good. I'll talk to the Sheriff in the morning and make sure he hasn't arranged our meeting with the Quinn family over the next couple of days."

The hotel we checked into adjoined Underground Atlanta and had an adjacent Marta subway stop. Jennifer would be able to shop to her heart's content while I was trying to interview Robert Svenson. The two of us had been here for a Southeastern Booksellers Association meeting to introduce one of my books several years earlier.

"You should have a reservation in the name of Shiloh Temple," I said to the desk clerk, a baby-faced young man who could have passed for fourteen. He tapped a few keys on his computer.

"Yes, we do. A single, business rate, with one double bed on the second floor, per your request for a lower floor."

"The room was supposed to be with *two* beds," I said.

"I'm sorry, there was apparently a misunderstanding. I can give you two double beds but the room would be on an upper floor."

"For God's sake, Shiloh," Jennifer said, "we can sleep in the same bed. I won't try to molest you."

The clerk's eyes opened wide and he quickly looked away.

"That room will all right," I said.

"Will you need a bellman?" the clerk asked.

"Yes, we will," Jennifer said before I could say anything. I had only my laptop computer and a medium bag, but she had three suitcases and a smaller bag for makeup and toiletries.

We went up to the room with the bellhop chattering inanely the entire way. Jennifer answered pleasantly, but I remained quiet. When I get a haircut I don't want the barber chattering, and when I'm eating out I don't want the server to be over-friendly. I'm always especially polite to service people, because I've done most jobs at one time or another, but pointless chitchat is not my thing.

"Thanks," the bellhop said as Jen handed him folded bills. I always forget how much I'm supposed to tip, but Jennifer knows about such things. "You folks have a good stay," the bellhop said as he closed the door.

"Shiloh, would you mind getting me some ice while I take a shower? I brought a bottle of Bailey's Irish Cream and I think I'll have a drink and take a nap," Jennifer said.

"Sure." I got the ice bucket and went looking for an ice machine. Bailey's Irish Cream is the only thing Jennifer drinks, and that very seldom.

The ice machine on our floor was out of order, as was the one on the third floor. I found one that actually had ice on the fourth floor and filled my bucket. I don't fear elevators or higher rooms, but I had been dumped from a hotel room by a fire alarm once and by the time I descended nine floors in the emergency stairwell, my heart was giving me problems. Ever since then, I had been careful to stay on the lower floors.

Back at our room, I inserted my electronic pass card and opened the door. As I stepped inside, Jennifer walked from the bathroom naked, a towel around her head. The sight of her body went through me like an electric shock. At thirty-eight, her body had aged very little from the girl I had fallen in love with. I turned my eyes away and put the ice bucket on the dresser. When I turned back around, she had a blue silk robe on.

"Sorry, Shiloh."

"It's no big deal," I said.

"Then why did you turn away?" she asked, unwinding the towel and shaking the mane of black hair around her shoulders.

"Staring is rude."

"I haven't been with another man since you left," she said, pulling a comb through her hair. "Have you been with another woman?"

"Why would I humiliate myself? You, on the other hand, should be moving on. There's nothing *wrong* with you."

"You're hopeless!" There was an edge to her voice.

"I think I'm going to run down my suspect," I said. "The last time he was interviewed, he was working the second shift at an electronics store over in Marietta, and his mother says he's still there. He may not let me in if I go to his apartment, but maybe I can convince him to sit down with me if I catch him in a place where he can't lock me out."

"All right," Jennifer said. "Do you want to eat out tonight or have room service?"

"I thought we might take a walk underground and eat at one of the little restaurants there. Unless there's some place you'd rather go."

"No, that's fine," she said. "I'll take a nap while you're gone, and maybe hit a couple of department stores."

When I was in Atlanta doing construction work in the late 1960s, just after high school, Marietta was actually a separate place from Atlanta — almost a rural area. I lived in a cheap apartment complex called The Pines with a couple of other workers. These days, there's no break at all and Marietta is a part of the great Atlanta urban sprawl.

Driving slowly, I watched for the mall where Robert Svenson worked. I passed it twice before noticing the sign by the entrance to the strip mall. Parking was scarce and I ended up walking almost a city block before arriving at the store.

Inside the store, I wandered around looking at the electronic marvels that had arisen over the last twenty years, until I spotted Svenson waiting on an elderly man. I watched him from the corner of my eye as I tinkered with a new laptop computer chained to a counter. I didn't have to wait long. When the old man left, Svenson came to me.

"Is there something I can help you with, sir?" Svenson asked.

"I hope so, Mister Svenson. I'm Lieutenant Shiloh Tempest and I just took over the task force that's investigating the murder of Cynthia Quinn and the assault on you."

"I told my mother I wouldn't come back Knoxville to be questioned again." He was smaller and slighter even than he had looked in the picture I had seen of him at the emergency room before the doctors began to stitch him up. His pale blue eyes had clouded with anger.

"And I don't blame you," I said. "You were treated very badly. So I came to you."

"There's a coffee shop two doors down, Lieutenant. If you'll wait there, I'll arrange to take my lunch break."

"I don't want to cause problems with your boss, Mister Svenson. We can meet when it's more convenient for you."

"I *am* the boss, Lieutenant, at least on this shift. I spent four years getting a degree in marketing so I could sell electronic gadgets. I'll be at the coffee shop in a few minutes. Turn right as you leave, two doors down."

It was a short walk to the coffee shop, a Starbuck's knockoff. I wondered if Svenson was going to rabbit on me. He didn't, though. We were soon sitting at a table. I was drinking regular coffee and he was having some type of frothy, coffee-based drink.

"I remain firm in my resolve not to return to Knoxville, Lieutenant, but you've come a long way. What is it you want to know?" Apparently Svenson was not a man to beat around the bush. I like that trait in a person.

"I was hoping you'd tell me who killed Cynthia Quinn."

"You don't mince words, do you, Lieutenant?" He took a sip of his drink, watching me over the top of the cup.

"Let's say I'm not very good at."

"If it hadn't been for Chief Rosenbaum, you'd already know *I* didn't kill Cynthia. As it is, I'm still under a cloud."

"Two things have changed: Robert. Rosenbaum was removed from the case --and there's no love lost between us— and nobody thinks you killed Cynthia. Personally, I think you loved her."

His eyes locked with mine. "On what do you base that theory?"

"When the first officer arrived on the scene, you told him your *girlfriend* had been stabbed. By the time you talked to the detectives, you were referring to her as your *roommate*."

"Did I, now? Maybe I was in shock and didn't know what I was saying."

"That's possible. *Were* you in love with Cynthia?" I asked, lighting a cigarette.

"May I have one of those, Lieutenant? I've been trying to quit without much success." I shook one out and lit it for him.

"*If* I had been in love with her, Lieutenant, it wouldn't have mattered. Cyn was a broken girl, trying to heal herself by sleeping with every man and woman who would do it. I was never one for standing in line."

"Did she ever tell you how she got broken, Robert?"

"No, but you know what sleepwalking, nightmares, and promiscuous behavior point to, Lieutenant?"

"Did Cynthia ever indicate she'd been abused?"

"No, but she was terrified of her uncle. That was easy enough to see." He took another sip of his adulterated coffee.

"Is it possible she gave Joshua Quinn a key to the apartment?"

"No, but her adopted mother had one."

"Was Joshua Quinn the man who stabbed you and Cynthia? Did he threaten your life if you gave him up?"

"Lieutenant Tempest, you write very good books. I take you to be a highly intelligent man. I am also an intelligent man, and if Joshua Quinn or anyone else threatened my life, do you think I'd put myself in further danger by telling you? Do you think I would have left my entire life behind if I'd thought I had a *real* choice? I have a family, too."

"If we knew who it was, Robert, we could lock him up and make sure he never hurt anyone else. It's not a perfect system, but that's how it is. With the investigation making progress, you may not be safe, anyway — assuming you know who he is."

"Lock him up first, Lieutenant Tempest, then we'll talk again — assuming I actually know anything that might help you. Thanks for the cappuccino."

"You've been quiet all morning," Jennifer said, as we left Marietta behind. "In fact, you had very little to say at dinner last night. What time did you finally come to bed?

"Just a lot on my mind, Jen. I finally dozed off around two in the morning. I was almost positive Svenson was going to tell me something yesterday afternoon. And here I am going back empty-handed."

"It wasn't a total loss. You said he convinced you *he* had nothing to do with the murder. So you've eliminated a suspect. Besides, we had fun, didn't we?" Jennifer turned her eyes from the interstate and looked directly at me.

"Keep your eyes on the road. I don't want to explain why a civilian was driving a county car when it was wrecked. But yes, it was fun, Jen."

"Do you find my body repulsive these days, Shiloh?"

"God no! Whatever gave you that idea?"

"You looked away from me when I was naked. You're very careful not to touch me or let any affection show in your eyes."

"Jen, we've been over this again and again. A relationship is an agreement between two people and I can't keep up my end of the bargain. You deserve a life with a younger man."

"You don't feel that way about your son. You went on bailing him out of financial difficulties long after he was eighteen." Her voice was rising in pitch.

"I didn't enter a contract with my son. He didn't ask to be my son and I didn't promise him anything. You and I made a bargain, and now I can't keep up my end. Not only am I sexually dysfunctional, but I'm dying."

"It was a *two-way* bargain we made, Tempest. You wouldn't have deserted me if I had come down with a fatal illness, but you want me to abandon you." Tears began to overflow her eyes and run down her face.

"Jen, pull over at the rest stop coming up. I knew it was a bad idea for me to move back in. It's getting complicated like it was before. I'm going to move back to my apartment when we get home, and you need to get on with your life."

I had every intention of moving out of Jen's house when we got home that day, then I found out my apartment building had burned down — in a fire accidentally set by homeless people camping in the vacant lot next door.

ELEVEN

The only insects buzzing around the apartment complex were carpenter bees. The dogwoods and other flowering trees had bloomed early, then a four day cold snap hit, killing buds and fragile new green leaves. It was warm again, but the trees had not yet begun to recover. Carpenter bees belong to a hardy species.

There were few signs of children in the complex where Cynthia Quinn had lived the last few months of her short life. I stood at the back of the apartment, on the spot where Cynthia's killer had left blood spatter when he fled. The wooden porches were all identical in either direction.

The back door of the apartment opened and a man in his early thirties stepped out, wearing only blue jeans. He was unshaven and bleary-eyed.

"Is there something I can help you with, or are you just out here scaring housewives?" he asked in a none-too-friendly tone.

Pushing my jacket back, I displayed the seven-pointed star on my belt.

"Sorry, officer. My wife saw you out here and woke me up."

"No problem," I said. "I'm sorry I inconvenienced you."

"Something happen out here today?" he asked.

"No, I'm investigating an old case."

"The girl who was stabbed to death in this apartment?"

"I didn't figure the owners would advertise that incident," I said.

"They didn't, but people talk. And after I found out, they lowered my rent. Good luck, officer, I'm going back to bed."

I had walked the possible routes that might have been taken by Cynthia's killer several times. In the week since my trip to Atlanta, Freed, Reagan and I had had fallen into a routine of meeting every morning for coffee to brainstorm and look at leads that were still trickling in — mainly because Joshua Quinn had posted a $50,000 reward.

He had put his cell phone number instead of ours on the billboards and flyers with Cynthia's picture and the composite drawing, so essentially he was screening the tips before we got most of them. If he had killed Cynthia, it was a good deal for him. The calls we got were usually from people who hadn't written down the number when they saw it on the billboard or flyers.

The next morning Sheriff Renfro and I would have our first face-to-face meeting with Joshua Quinn and his wife, Cynthia's aunt and uncle by blood and daughter by adoption after both her parents had died in a car wreck when she was two. Freed and Reagan would be there and Rosenbaum had *demanded* to be there, but the Sheriff had turned him down because I said I'd quit if he was present.

As I walked back to my car, a small white pickup truck with an amber dash light and *Security* painted in black letters on the door pulled up. A big man in his late fifties or early sixties got out. He was wearing khakis, had a Model 1911 .45 on his hip and a badge that said *Security Officer*.

"Podnuh, I need to ask why you're prowlin' around the complex," he said.

"Walking around in broad daylight doesn't exactly qualify as prowling —
Pod-nuh."

He was bright enough to understand my ill-concealed contempt. A scowl passed over his face and he walked towards me. As he got closer, I saw that his hair was of the shade that had always rated the nickname *Whitey* when I was growing up in the Lonsdale and Beaumont sections of Knoxville. His eyes were a pale watery-blue and his eyebrows and eyelashes were the same shade as his hair. He paused less than a foot from me, towering over me by several inches.

"Mister, I asked you a polite question and I expect a polite answer."

"You step back about two feet or I'm going to *politely* put your big ass in jail for assault and check to see if you have a permit to carry that hog's leg on your belt."

He stepped back quickly, the starch going right out of him.

"That's better. I'm Lieutenant Shiloh Tempest from the sheriff's department. Who are you? Break out some ID."

Fumbling with his wallet, he kept glancing at me. I had not shown any identification at that point. A police officer who learns to use *the voice* never forgets. The shorter an officer, the more attitude he or she needs to acquire. I have plenty.

Finally, he extended a special deputy card. From the colored strip across the top, I saw that he was deputized only to carry a weapon on the premises where he worked.

"I'm sorry, Lieutenant. I'm the maintenance chief and security officer here at the complex. I should've identified myself." He didn't point out that he was in a vehicle clearly marked *Security*.

"David Gettlefinger, you should learn some manners. Just because you can get away with throwing your weight around doesn't mean you should."

I handed his card back then showed him my credentials and the star on my belt, so I could say I had, if asked. "How long have you been working here, Gettlefinger?"

"A little over five years, Lieutenant. I came to check on you because somebody saw you and called the office."

"Then I suppose you were questioned in the Cynthia Quinn case — since you have a master key to every apartment."

"Lieutenant, I know we got off to a bad start, but I'm a God fearin' man and I ain't never been in trouble. Yeah, they questioned me but I was in bed asleep when the sirens woke me up that night."

"I didn't suggest you had anything to do with her death. I just asked a question. What I do want to know is whether you ever had complaints at Cynthia's apartment or if you ever knew of her calling the police for any reason."

"We had a couple of calls about loud music, but the manager just sent them a letter askin' for them to quiet down a little. Only time I ever knew of the police bein' here was when somebody broke into Cynthia's car."

"When was that?"

"A couple of months before she was killed," Gettlefinger said. "Lieutenant, can I smoke a cigarette? I'm a little nervous here."

"Help yourself. I'm not the health police. Did you tell the detectives who interviewed you about the car break-in?"

"No, it was such a minor incident, I didn't think about it." He lit a non-filtered cigarette and his hands were shaking.

"All right, Mister Gettlefinger, thanks for the information."

He sighed with relief and almost jogged back to his pickup truck. The world is full of want-to-be police officers and bullies. Very often they are one and the same. I pondered what I had learned all the way back to headquarters, then went directly to the records division.

"Shiloh, it's true you're *back*— and I'm devastated you didn't come to see me first thing." The speaker was Tasha Abernathy and she had joined the sheriff's department as a clerk when I was a detective. A tall, gorgeous brunette, she had engaged in a little harmless flirtation with me. When we would meet in the halls and stop to chat, Tasha would lean against the wall and begin to slide down, apparently because she was self-conscious about being nearly six feet tall and thought I was uncomfortable with being short.

"Tasha, I didn't want the rumors about our being lovers to start again. Besides, I thought you would have moved on to bigger and better things."

"Well, I *am* second in command over records now. How can I help you?"

"This department has a special deputy by the name of David Gettlefinger. I need everything you can find on him. Also, I need to know if Cynthia Quinn filed a police report of any kind between February the first and April the ninth, two years ago."

"Your wish is my command, Lieutenant Shiloh Tempest. Give me about ten minutes." She disappeared into the depths of the record division and I stood at the counter waiting until Sam Renfro went by and saw me. He turned around and came back.

"Whas'up, Dawg?" he said, extending his hand. He was wearing a pale blue seersucker suit, a dark blue shirt and a tie to match the suit. His shoes were buckskin suede.

"Not much, Homeboy. I've been running down leads." A couple of patrol officers walked by just as I was referring to the Sheriff as "Homeboy," and looked puzzled because they obviously didn't know me.

"Are you turning up anything substantial? Maybe something we can tell Joshua and Emma Quinn when they come in tomorrow morning?"

"We can tell them we have some new leads on a couple of suspects, but I don't think we need to tell him he's one of the suspects."

"I guess not, Hoss. I'll see you in the morning. Don't be late." Sam punched me lightly on the shoulder and left.

"It's good to see you and Sam working together again, Shiloh," Tasha said from behind the counter. "Gettlefinger has had two complaints. A female tenant said she thought he had a camera concealed in her apartment because he had mentioned something he shouldn't have known about. Internal affairs searched her apartment and didn't find one. A male complainant said Gettlefinger roughed him up, but IA couldn't confirm that, either.

"Cynthia Quinn filed a complaint that her vehicle had been broken into on February the sixth, two years ago. I made copies of everything for you." She handed me a manila envelope.

"I hear you and Jennifer are separated, Shiloh. Does that mean I might have a shot at you now?" She raised her eyebrows in a mock salacious manner.

"Only if you can raise the dead, Tasha. Thanks."

"I could *try*," she said as I waved to her and headed down to my office.

As I unlocked the office door, I smelled fresh coffee. Reagan was sitting at his desk with two Polaroid pictures in front of him. "Didn't expect to see you here this late in the afternoon," he said. I found two of the men that came in on the tip line and Freed is running down another one in East Knox County."

"Either of yours look promising?" I asked, going to the table behind Reagan's desk to pour myself what was obviously fresh coffee. I poured him a cup, too, then put a sugar cube in mine and handed him his, black.

"Thanks, Loo. You don't really put much faith in the composite drawing do you?"

"No, I really don't, Reagan, but we have to keep running the tips down."

"Now that you've talked to the roommate, Svenson, you seem to have lost interest in the composite altogether. He convinced you of something, Loo. What was it?"

"He convinced me he's innocent and too scared to speak up. It follows that the composite he gave was pulled out of his ass in self-defense."

"It may be the case, Lieutenant."

"Do you remember interviewing this guy?" I handed him the special deputy application with Gettlefinger's picture on it.

"Yeah, we interviewed him, but since he was known to Svenson and Svenson didn't finger him, we didn't push too hard."

"Take a look at these." I gave Reagan the internal affairs report.

He looked them over and whistled. "Loo, it looks like you can do more detective work in a couple of weeks than we've done in two years."

"Don't beat yourself up. You and Freed have done a good job, but nobody catches everything. How about this? Did it turn up in the initial investigation?"

He took the report on the break-in of Cynthia Quinn's car and examined it. "No, but we should have had a copy. We pulled all the back reports for a year from that complex and this one wasn't there."

"When patrol writes a report, who gets copies?" I asked.

"One goes to records, one goes to the analyst and the other comes down here, where shift supervisors review them and assign them to a detective if there's any solvability at all.

"I suppose Chief Rosenbaum reviews them before the shift supervisors get them. But whether it was assigned to a detective or not, it should have been in our master files, and it wasn't," Reagan said, taking a sip of coffee. "Things do fall through the cracks, Loo."

"Yes, they do, Detective. Tomorrow, right after the interview with the Quinn, I'm going to try and contact the complainants. I want to see if there was any truth to the tenant's complaint about a camera in her apartment."

"Do you know this Officer Bumbalough who did the report on Cynthia Quinn's break-in?" I asked, taking a deep swallow of hot, black coffee.

"Yeah, I know the Bumble Bee." Reagan said with a smile. "Got the nickname because of his first year out. In one year, his cruiser blew an engine because one of the garage technicians forgot to put oil back in when he changed it; a crane dropped a headache ball on his *new* cruiser at a crime scene; and a meth freak shot him in the arm as he got out to help the guy with a flat tire. He's been good since then, though."

"All right, Detective Reagan. I'll see you in the Sheriff's office in the morning for refreshments with the Quinns."

"Loo, what will we do if Joshua Quinn passes on all the refreshments again?"

"We'll do what good cops always do," I replied. "We'll improvise."

TWELVE

"**Sheriff, just give** me one good reason why you won't let that television show run Cynthia's case." Joshua Quinn was as obnoxious in person as he had appeared on the numerous television appearances he had made. A big, beefy man of fifty-eight years, whose hair was still mostly black. A former U.S. Naval captain, in the habit of being obeyed.

"Mister Quinn," Sam Renfro said patiently, "I don't know how to make it any clearer. The FBI, all my detectives and Lieutenant Tempest, who was kind enough to come out of retirement to take over this investigation, think it's a bad idea.

"We believe the suspect is still in the area and if we go national, he might get scared and run. If he does flee the area, our chances of catching him drop nearly to zero."

"It's been over two years and you're no closer to finding our daughter's killer than you were when it happened." He pursed his lips and looked at the array of bottled water for perhaps the tenth time since we had sat down at the Sheriff's conference table. He was obviously thirsty, but just as obviously had no intention of taking a drink.

"Sir, that's just not true. We've investigated and eliminated dozens of suspects. If you would put *our* number on the billboards, flyers and television spots you're running, it would help a great deal," Sam Renfro said.

"I'm *paying* for all of those things and I don't intend to have the leads tossed on a desk and forgotten about," Quinn snapped. "When was the last time you even talked to Cynthia's roommate?"

"No lead is tossed aside," Sam said, "and sometimes the manner in which a caller speaks is as important as the information itself. Killers tend to be fascinated by their own cases and our detectives are trained to look for signs. As for your question, Lieutenant Tempest interviewed Robert Svenson a few days ago. He's working at an electronics store in Marietta, Georgia."

"The hell you say, Sheriff. I think a five-year-old child could have solved this case by now — assuming he was actually *doing* something!"

"Josh, try to keep your voice down," his wife Emma said, sipping from a bottle of water she had taken from the ample selection of drinks. She was what my father would have called "a mousy woman," pretty but almost invisible in a group.

"Don't interrupt, Emma. This is man-to-man talk between me and the Sheriff. And you're right, Sheriff, I wasn't in law enforcement, but I was in Naval Intelligence. I commanded hundreds of men — every one of them asked *how high* when I said *jump*. Any leader worth his salt can do the same." Quinn's face had grown flushed.

"You had thirty years in the Navy, didn't you, Mister Quinn?" I asked.

"That's true, Lieutenant," he said, appearing somewhat puzzled. He had been working up a head of steam and I had distracted him.

"And you were an Annapolis graduate?" I continued.

"Yes, but what do these questions have to do with my daughter's murder?"

"Nothing, really. I was just wondering why a graduate of the U.S. Naval academy with thirty years of service got so close but never made admiral?"

It was like throwing a light switch. I had hit the rawest nerve in Quinn's body. So I pushed another button: "Did you know, Mister Quinn, that sleep-walking, nightmares and promiscuity are all signs of childhood abuse? Cynthia had all those symptoms. Is it possible you didn't get your admiral's star because you have anger management problems?"

"Shiloh, what the hell are you doing?" Sam hissed at me.

Quinn was on his feet by that time and I twisted the knife again. "Is that why Cynthia slept with a knife and dead-bolted the door at night. Was she afraid of the big, bad, swaggering, and *failed* naval captain who raised her?"

Before anyone else could react, Quinn was around the table and lunging for my throat with a guttural sound that could have come from an enraged animal. But I was also on my feet and before his hands touched me, I drove my right palm upward into his nose — not hard enough to kill him, but enough to spray blood all over the white shirt I had worn especially for the occasion.

The pain overcame his rage and he began to stagger. Reagan and Freed were on their feet, supporting him before he could fall.

"Reagan, Freed, get him out to the lobby and call an ambulance," the Sheriff said, opening the door to his office.

Just outside the sheriff's door, Chief Tim Rosenbaum was standing, his hand raised as if to knock. The suddenly-opened door had obviously startled him, but he recovered quickly. "I heard the ruckus and was about to see if you needed help, Sheriff."

"Help get Mister Quinn to the lobby and into an ambulance," the Sheriff said.

"Yes, sir." Rosenbaum slid his right shoulder under Quinn's right arm to support him. For a moment, both of them were staring directly at me with almost the same malevolent expression. Fortunately, looks cannot kill. The three officers and Joshua Quinn, followed by Emma Quinn, quickly vanished down the hallway.

When we were alone, Sam closed his door slowly, as if being careful not to slam it. He took a seat at his desk, opened a drawer and set a cheap metal ashtray in front of him. "Shiloh, give me a cigarette, please."

"You quit fifteen years ago, Sam," I said, extending my pack of Camel filters to him.

Sam took a cigarette, reached into his desk drawer again and came out with a butane lighter. He lit the cigarette and took a deep drag.

"I did quit, Shiloh and it *was* fifteen years ago. But I've kept this old metal ashtray and a lighter at my desk the whole time I've been off nicotine – as a reminder just in case I relapsed. The day one of my closest friends decided to get my department sued seemed a good time to relapse."

He took another drag before continuing. "Shiloh, I am now going to ask you, as calmly as possible, *why* you pushed Joshua Quinn over the edge and seriously injured him?"

"I was improvising, Sam. It became clear he was not going to drink anything, even though he was obviously thirsty. I needed a DNA sample and now I have it all over my shirt."

"Shiloh…" he started to speak, shook his head with a wry grin, then took another drag off his cigarette.

"He's not *really* hurt, Sam. I held back."

Sam chuckled and laid his head back on the headrest of the plush leather chair. "You and I did some really outrageous things when we were working together, but you just topped all of them in one fell swoop."

"Do you want my star, Sam? It would probably go a long way towards calming Joshua Quinn."

"No, Shiloh, I want the case solved. For future reference, though, if there's something you want and can't get any other way, just resort to illegal wire-tapping or breaking and entering — something easier to explain than beating up on a victim's father."

"Sam, to be truthful, I don't think he'll sue *or* go to the media. He just got his ass kicked by a fifty-nine-year-old with a bad heart, who barely comes to his shoulder and weighs a hundred pounds less."

"You may be right. I'll tell him that when I remind him that he's the one who attacked you. Because the emergency room is where I'll be until Joshua Quinn is released.

"Take your shirt on to forensics. It takes a long time to get a DNA sample back. And send someone out to get you a fresh shirt."

"I brought an extra shirt, Sam."

"Of course you did, Shiloh. Now, if you'll excuse me, I'm going to compose myself and head over to whichever emergency room they're taking Quinn."

"By the way, Sam, that's a nice navy blue suit. You must have a closet full of nice clothes. Okay, I'm on my way out. Don't get up."

Outside the Sheriff's office, I walked through the lobby to the elevators. An ambulance was backed up to the main doors and Joshua Quinn was being loaded. The usual crowd had gathered, and probably for the same reason people once gathered at the Coliseum in Rome --to view whatever carnage had occurred, first hand.

Reagan and Freed were already back at their desks when I entered the office. They looked up expectantly. "Hope you're not here to clean out your desk, Loo," Freed said.

"Nope, I just need a large evidence bag."

"I'll get one," Reagan said. He put down his coffee and lumbered out of the office.

When I opened my desk drawer and took out a clean shirt, my regular plaid in green, Freed smiled. "Looks like you might have been expecting to get your shirt dirty today, Lieutenant."

"You just never know when a suspect will go berserk and attack you, Freed." I took off my bloody shirt and folded it.

"Loo, you have some nasty-looking scars," Freed said.

"Coronary bypass surgery and drainage tubes. The fresh one is where the defibrillator box went in and the one on back was from a hawksbill knife. I have a scar on my ass, too, but you don't want to see that," I told him, slipping on my clean shirt.

Reagan returned with an evidence bag that looked a lot like an ordinary bag used by grocery stores before plastic. I put the shirt and my tie in it, sealed it shut with evidence tape and initialed it, dated and put the time on it to protect the chain of evidence.

"Freed, if you will take this up to forensics."

"Gotcha covered, Loo." He took the bag and left the office.

"That was one hell of an evidence-collecting technique this morning," Reagan said. "It's not one they teach at the academy."

"I told you I'd improvise if I had to." I finished buttoning my shirt, tucked it in and fixed myself a cup of coffee. "How'd you two manage to get back down here so fast?"

"Rosenbaum sent us away as soon as we got to the lobby. I couldn't hear what he was telling the Quinns as we walked away, but I'm sure it was about you and I'm sure it wasn't complimentary."

"I'm sure it wasn't."

"By the way, Loo, here's the address and phone number of the woman who complained that Gettlefinger had been spying on her. She listed her mother as a contact and I called after you left yesterday evening. Mom gave me her new address and phone number. She's now married and has a baby." He handed me a slip of paper with the name and address on it.

"You're on the ball, Reagan. Have you called her?"

"No, I thought I'd pass it on to you. If it was something really embarrassing that Gettlefinger is supposed to have seen, I figured a more father-like figure — such as yourself — might have better luck talking to her."

"Al, are you yanking your lieutenant's chain?" I asked.

"No, Shiloh, just trying to be honest." I could see he was waiting for a reaction to his use of my first name, and when none came, he seemed to relax.

"You're probably right. You and John follow whatever leads you have available and I'll see if I can catch Tiffany Burke at home."

"It's now Tiffany Burke-Witt," Reagan said as I headed out the door.

Tiffany had apparently married well. The sprawling rancher was way above most starter homes. It was fully bricked and the landscaping looked profession-al. I pushed the doorbell and looked around as I waited. A Dachshund came around the house and approached me wagging his tail, quite unusual for a breed developed to pull badgers out of holes.

"What's up, pooch?"

The door opened and a young woman with a baby in her arms looked out with a quizzical expression. She was bleached blonde, professionally done, but the hair didn't match her dark complexion.

"Lieutenant Shiloh Tempest," I held up my star. "Are you Tiffany Burke-Witt?"

"Yes, I am. Is something wrong?"

"No, I'm following up on a complaint you made about David Gettlefinger."

"That was over two years ago. Has the creep done something else?"

"That's what I'm trying to determine. I wonder if I might come in and talk to you."

"All right, come on in. I was getting ready to feed my baby. I can talk while I'm doing it." She unlocked the storm door and walked away. I followed her, noticing that she was apparently in good shape. Probably a little heavier than she wanted to be, but nice just the same. A man is alive as long as he still looks.

"Have a seat at the kitchen table. There's coffee if you want it. The cups are in the cabinet above the sink." She put the baby, which looked to be about a year old, in a high chair and strapped it in.

"Thank you, but I'll pass on the coffee. I appreciate your time," I said, sit-ting down in a wooden kitchen chair.

"No problem. If there's anything I can do to cause David Gettlefinger problems, I'll be glad to help." She gave the baby a spoonful of some kind of green food and the baby made a face before swallowing.

"In the complaint you filed, you told the detectives you thought Gettlefinger had a camera hidden in your apartment. What exactly made you believe that?"

"You can't tell by looking at the size of my butt now, but I studied dance for twelve years. In the privacy of my apartment, I used to work out and dance nude. The first time he made a remark to me about 'nude dancing,' I put up new Venetian blinds and heavy drapes. When he brought it up again and said something about 'long-legged ballerinas,' I knew he was watching me some other way.

"After I thought about it awhile, I went to the security office and caught him looking at the monitors. Most of the monitors showed the outside of the apartments, but he turned off a separate monitor when I entered and I was *sure* I saw the inside of an apartment on that screen.

"He denied it, and the next morning I stopped by the office and told the manager I was going to call the police, which I did, of course.

At some point that day, Gettlefinger got the camera out. I could have kicked myself for telling the manager *before* I called the sheriff's department." She fed the baby another spoonful of the noxious-looking green stuff.

"Were there other incidents of a similar nature that you heard about, while you were living in that complex?"

"Oh yeah. All the women complained about Gettlefinger *accidentally* walking in while they were dressing or stepping out of the shower. One girl's boyfriend confronted him and they had a fight."

"Tiffany, would you be willing to testify to what you've told me if I make a case against Gettlefinger?"

"You can bet your ass I would," she said. "Most women were too scared to confront that creep, but I wasn't and I'm not."

THIRTEEN

Jennifer was sitting at her writing desk in the sunroom, staring out the window despite an open folder in front of her. She looked up and smiled when I came in. "I saw on the television news that there was a ruckus at the sheriff's department. What do you know about that?"

"I was attacked by a distraught father during an interview. That's my story and I'm sticking to it because it's true."

"That's what Sheriff Sam said during his interview, but an *unnamed* source inside the sheriff's department has hinted at a rogue cop deliberately provoking an incident. Are you going to need a civil lawyer?" Jennifer asked.

"The unnamed source would be Rosenbaum, I'd say. No, I don't think I need a lawyer because I don't think the distraught father actually *wants* anyone to know what happened."

"Well, if you need an attorney, you know my number," she said.

"What are you working on?" I asked.

"It's Josie Fletcher's case. My pretrial motions to throw out her initial confession and to downgrade her charge to voluntary manslaughter were dismissed today. We go to trial Monday."

For a moment, I saw the twenty-year-old I had first seen at the University of Tennessee, still fresh from an abusive relationship, but willing to take a risk for a relationship of the kind she wanted — to a point. That's why we had never officially gotten married.

"I know you'll do your best," I said. "And I know how important it is to you."

"It's hitting close to home, Shiloh." she said. "There but for the Grace of God and all that, I could easily have been Josie Fletcher. I only put up with the abuse for a year. I don't know what I might have done if it had gone on much longer."

There didn't seem to be a satisfactory reply, so I didn't make one.

The woman behind the desk, who had gray hair with a bluish tint that was once popular with middle-aged women but is seldom seen today, looked up at me, Freed and Reagan and said, "How can I help you, gentlemen?"

"We're from the sheriff's department and we have a search warrant for your security room. Are you the manager?" I showed her my identification and handed her a copy of the search warrant.

"I'm the manager, but I'll have to insist on having our attorney present if you're going to search here." She reached for the telephone.

"Sorry," Reagan said. "You can call your attorney, if you like, but meanwhile we'll be searching. A search warrant wouldn't be very effective if everyone had a say in how and when it was executed. We need you to open the door to the security room or we'll have to kick it in."

"This is outrageous," the woman said, but handed Reagan a key.

"We also need to know David Gettlefinger's whereabouts at the moment. We have a search warrant for his apartment, but he gets that warrant, not you," I said.

"He's somewhere in the complex," she said. "There are three-hundred units and he could be at any of them. I may have to cooperate until I get my attorney out here, but I don't have to show you where David's apartment is. This is the United States."

"That's all right, we know his apartment number and there are officers watching it and his vehicle right now," I told her. "How many people have access to the security room?"

"David's the only one allowed in there. He handles all security and supervises four maintenance men. I have a key, obviously, but I have no reason to go in there. Just how did you get his apartment number, anyway?" the blue-haired lady asked sharply.

"Ma'am," Freed said. "We have access to some of the same tools as the Central Intelligence Agency and the Federal Bureau of Investigation. We have phonebooks and city directories."

"Get on the radio and alert the officers watching the apartment and pickup truck, and tell them Gettlefinger's out in the complex on foot, Freed," I said. "And tell the tech guy to come on in. Let everyone know Gettlefinger is probably armed with at least a handgun, a 1911 Colt .45 caliber, as a matter of fact.

"Let's take a look at the cameras, Reagan."

Reagan unlocked the door to the security room, just off the main office. There was a bank of monitors, some fixed on specific places, such as the entrance to the complex, others were going off and on in sequence, all recording what they picked up. There were switches to stop a particular monitor wherever the operator wanted to focus.

"Loo, there's a laptop computer separate from the main bank of cameras hooked up to a monitor that's not part of the main system. It's recording right now."

"That's what Tiffany said she saw. Don't touch anything until the technician gets here," I said.

As if on cue, a young man in jeans and white Nike running shoes, wearing a knit shirt with the sheriff's department emblem on it, came through the door. He looked like a teenager, though I was sure he wasn't. "You rang?" he said. "I'm Todd Culvahouse. What're we looking for?"

"First, tell us what this camera is recording," Reagan said.

The technician went over and stood in front of the monitor and laptop for a few seconds, then hit a key on the computer and the screen came alive. A young woman in a robe was bathing a child.

"This is an amateur set-up," the technician said. "The camera isn't bad, probably cost a few hundred. The picture's coming in on an electronic feed, recording to a disk in the computer."

"Can you tell where the signal's coming from?" I asked.

"Ordinarily I'd have to use some specific equipment, but I think there may be a shortcut. He punched a button on the side of the computer and the disk popped out. Leaning over, he read the hand-written script, apparently inscribed with a felt-tipped marker on the disk. "It's coming from apartment 27-A and it should be someone named Shelia Andrews."

"Al, you and Todd go to apartment 27-A, see if the tenant will let you re-trieve the camera and see if she'll prosecute. If she refuses, tell her how long you'll be in her apartment before someone brings a warrant. Bag the camera for forensics to check for fingerprints. I'll take Freed with me to Gettlefinger's apartment. We'll need an officer to secure this security room until we're finished."

Back in the main office, I stopped in front of the blue-haired woman's desk. "I need the key to Gettlefinger's apartment."

"I won't give it to you," she said.

"Suit yourself, "I said. "You can pay for the damage to the door." We turned to leave and she had a change of heart.

"Here's the key," she said. "But I'm giving it to you under protest."

"Protest noted," I said, taking the key from her hand.

Outside Gettlefinger's apartment, Freed and I drew our weapons, just in case he had been inside when we arrived. The officers who were watching Gettlefinger's apartment and vehicle nodded and waved to us from their positions at the end of the building, where they could see both the back and front doors.

The two of us button-hooked through the doors, left and right, covering each other, and repeated it at every other door until we were certain he wasn't there. Then we slipped on latex gloves and looked around.

"This place is a pig-sty, Loo," Freed said. "The sink looks like he never did dishes. The place is covered with fast food wrappers and boxes, and that bathroom is so toxic it worries me. And he has the largest collection of porno-graphy I ever seen stacked by his bed and his easy chair."

"Yes, but there is one neat spot in the room," I said.

It was a standing case filled with computer disks in identical plastic holders, each neatly hand-labeled on the spine, all of them in alphabetical order. I went down to "Q" and found what I was looking for. It was labeled *Apartment 22-D, Cynthia Quinn.* I didn't touch it. I wanted all the evidence in pristine condition for the forensics unit.

Outside, as we were taking breaths of fresh air, Reagan and the technician pulled up in our county-issue Chevrolet compact. They got out of the car, carrying an evidence bag with the camera inside. Reagan didn't look pleased.

"Loo, one of the tenants just stopped us and asked if we were looking for Gettlefinger. She said he was working on a light switch in her apartment when we pulled in and the last time she saw him he was running across the tennis court into the trees towards Kingston Pike. Do you want to put the bird in the air?"

"No, I can't justify using the helicopter on what's essentially a low-grade felony right now. Put out a BOLO for him. He'll turn up. By the time forensics is finished here and Todd examines Gettlefinger's computer, maybe we'll have something more serious to charge him with."

"You've generated a lot of attention from the media over the last two days, Hoss. They know I have a famous crime novelist working the Quinn case and are dying to run with the story. Do you want to give any interviews?" Sam Renfro, asked, leaning back in the leather chair.

"Absolutely not. As a matter of fact, I'm going to take two or three personal days and I'll be out pocket for a while. Assuming you have no objections."

"Going on a trip?" Sam asked.

"Yes, I am."

"Is it related to the investigation?"

"That depends on what I find. If you don't mind, while I'm gone, I'd like to have you discreetly order a copy of the tape from our incident in your office yesterday and get me copies of the original vacation requests for every officer in the department for the week of Cynthia Quinn's murder. I don't want focus put on a single individual. Make it look like routine bookkeeping."

"You'd better give me a cigarette, Shiloh," the Sheriff said.

I shook a cigarette out of my pack and Sam took it. He removed the metal ashtray and butane lighter from his desk drawer again, then lit the cigarette and took a deep drag. I noticed that his suit was a pale gray and his shirt a pastel yellow.

"You're looking at someone in *my* department for the Quinn murder."

"Among several individuals," I said, lighting a cigarette for myself.

"Suppose I order you to give me the name?"

"Sam, you know how well I take orders. There's no reason for me to plant seeds of doubt in this department unless I find more than I have now."

"So you're not going to tell me who you're looking at?"

"Not unless you insist — and I hope you won't. The case is moving and I'm confident we'll solve it. But I don't want anyone to know where I'm going. I'll put it on my personal credit card and bill the department later.

"I'll have Reagan and Freed stonewall any questions about my whereabouts. By the time I get back, forensics will hopefully have things to report and that young techie, Culvahouse, will have analyzed the hard drive of David Gettlefinger's computer."

"When are you leaving?" Sam asked.

"In the morning. First, I'm going to make sure the disks we seized today are what we think they are."

"Have a good trip. Try not to end up on the six o'clock news, wherever it is you're going," the Sheriff said with a chuckle.

Downstairs in our cramped little office, I found Freed and Reagan watching a video on a portable player. "Take a look, Loo," Reagan said. "Forensics dusted the Quinn disk for prints first and Todd burned us a copy. Forensics is lifting prints from the rest of them and we'll get them as soon as they're copied.

In the video, Cynthia Quinn could be seen moving in and out of the bathroom in her bra and panties. There were abrupt breaks, indicating that parts of it had been edited out. She left the bathroom and returned with a towel, took off her undergarments and stepped into the shower, looking even more waif-like than in the crime scene photos I had seen.

"That slimy bastard has been doing this for years," Freed said. "Todd says the later videos are of a better quality than earlier ones, but he thinks Gettlefinger was only set up for one camera at a time and kept moving it from one apartment to another."

"Turn off the video. We need to talk," I said.

"Sure, Loo. There's nothing wrong, is there?" Reagan asked. His round face wrinkled in concern.

"No, nothing's wrong. I'm going out of town for a couple of days and I don't want anyone else but you two and the Sheriff to know it."

"Not a problem, Loo. We'll cover for you," Freed said.

"We already have two living victims. I want you to get warrants for Gettle-finger and have the two victims sign off. That will give us something to hold him on if he surfaces before I get back. You also need to get a warrant for the tenant records from the apartment complex to identify other victims by apartment numbers, because I don't think the manager's going to cooperate.

"If you can, sit tight on this case until I get back, but do whatever you think is necessary if something unexpected surfaces. It's your case."

"You sure you don't want backup on your trip?" Reagan asked.

"No, I won't be in any danger. You guys hold the fort down. Keep your cell phones on and so will I."

FOURTEEN

I hate flying. When the plane finally touches down, it's as if all the muscles in my body suddenly begin to unravel, leaving me weak for a few minutes. I've never really had a bad flight, other than routine turbulence, but I spend *every* flight holding the plane in the air by force of will.

It's only when I can't justify the time it would take to drive someplace that I get on a plane. I'm always glad to be back on the ground. If my destination is within two hundred miles, I always drive. Otherwise, I get on an airplane and spend time pretending I'm not terrified.

It's hard to believe I once jumped out of airplanes for a living. Well, actually, I never jumped in combat, but I trained for it. When I finally saw combat with the 173rd Light Infantry Brigade in the Republic of Vietnam, it was to spend two days inching up Hill 875 near Dak Tho. I was scared then, but not a lot more scared than I am on an airliner.

The compact department Chevrolet came up the access road beside the McGhee Tyson airport, which is actually in Blount County, but is operated on some kind of lease deal by adjoining Knox County. I saw that Reagan was driving. He looked grim, but he always does. The big detective popped the trunk from inside and got out to help me put my luggage in the trunk.

"Hey, Loo. Have a good trip?" Reagan inquired.

"As good as any trip can be when you're on an aircraft that's heavier than air and prone to falling out of the sky."

"Don't like flying, I take it, Loo?"

"Not at all, Detective Reagan. Not at all. Any breaks in our case?" I asked, closing the trunk.

"Maybe. There was a message in our box this morning from Robert Svenson. He wants you to call him as soon as possible. It came in after we left yesterday. Since we knew you'd be arriving home this morning, we decided it was best to wait on you. In Svenson's mind, John and I are the bad cops."

"What about Gettlefinger?"

"One of his cousins saw the television news story about him and called in that he thinks Gettlefinger stole his car the day we served the search warrant."

"Why does he think it's our boy?"

"Gettlefinger sold him the car and the victim assumes he kept keys. It was an old Oldsmobile, so it isn't likely that anybody would steal it for fun or profit — and it was taken from a location only a couple of miles from the apartment complex.

"We have a BOLO on Gettlefinger *and* the car now. We can assume he has transportation. His cousin said the car was in rough shape on the outside but runs real well."

"Have you identified any of the other victims on Gettlefinger's CD collection yet?"

"No. Culvahouse has them all copied and he's digging into the hard drive of the laptop now. There were over a hundred disks. And Culvahouse says most of them were originally recorded on other disks and transferred to the ones we have so Gettlefinger could edit out the non-action segments. So far, all the prints from the disks belong to Gettlefinger."

"You mind if I smoke in your car, Al?"

"Naw, go ahead. I used to be a smoker myself,"

"You look like you might have gotten a little sun, Loo — wherever you were." He cast a glance in my direction but I let it pass.

"What else do we know about Gettlefinger now?" I asked.

"Believe it or not, he was a career Marine with no blemishes that we could find on his service records. The only thing in the system, besides the original complaint about the camera, is the one complaint from the guy who said Gettlefinger roughed him up. We tracked him down and he said his girlfriend had accused Gettlefinger of spying on her, and that was the reason for the dustup.

"That would have been the one Tiffany Burke-Witt told me about when I interviewed her. Go ahead, didn't mean to interrupt."

"Gettlefinger grew up in Union County, graduated from high school there, then went into the Marines. Oh yeah, he was wounded in the first Gulf War, but not seriously."

"Our boy never got past buck sergeant. When he was passed over the last time, he got out. Ever since, he's worked menial jobs. Security and maintenance at the apartment complex is the most responsible position he's had since leaving the Corps.

"That fits the FBI profile, Loo. They said our killer would probably be someone who worked at a menial job."

"That it does, Al. That it does. We'll know when we get his DNA — or a confession."

"Loo, did you want to go home and get your car or go straight to headquarters?" Reagan asked.

"Let's go to headquarters. I need to call Robert Svenson back and I want to get it on audio in case he blurts something out."

John Freed was puppy-dog-glad to see me. He seemed to be a carefree, laid-back individual, or at least he did until I found out he had been married three times and was single again. People are not always as cheerful they seem. But he comes across as a dedicated cop and that's all a police supervisor can ask.

"Good to see you, Lieutenant. Did you solve the case while you were gone?"

"No, Freed, I'm sorry. It looks like we'll just have to keep working together for a while," I answered.

"I can handle that, Loo. Where's Al?"

"I think he stopped to take a leak, John."

"Well, all right, then. Did Al catch you up-to-date on Gettlefinger?"

"Yes, he did. Will you rig my phone up so I can record my conversation with Robert Svenson?"

While Freed was working on the telephone, I poured myself a cup of stale coffee. By the time I added sugar and took my first bitter sip, the phone connection was rigged. "Here's Svenson's number, Loo."

The phone rang four times before it was answered and the voice didn't belong to Svenson. "Hello."

"This is Lieutenant Shiloh Tempest from the sheriff's office in Knox County, Tennessee. I'm returning a call from Robert Svenson."

"This is Sergeant Roy Johnson with the Marietta Police Department. Is your connection with Svenson personal or professional?"

"He's a witness in one of our cases," I responded.

"Not any more, Lieutenant. Someone killed him last night. We're working the crime scene now."

"What can you tell me about it?" I asked.

"Nothing over the phone, Lieutenant. If you want to come down here, we'll share information. Just ask for Sergeant Roy Johnson."

"I'll do that. Look for me tomorrow, Sergeant."

"What was your name again, Lieutenant?

"Tempest, Shiloh Tempest." I put the phone down.

"What's wrong, Loo? You look like white as a bed sheet on laundry day," Freed said.

"Robert Svenson has been killed. I'm going home to take a shower and pack. You or Reagan turn in a new request to Chief Rosenbaum for me to take the vehicle assigned to me out of state. If he squawks, call the Sheriff.

"Oh yeah, and we need to know the whereabouts of Joshua Quinn yesterday. And if Gettlefinger is picked up while I'm gone, call me. Make sure he doesn't get out on bond before I'm back."

Jennifer pulled into the driveway of her house just as the patrol officer I had caught a ride with dropped me off. She left the garage door open until I carried my luggage in. I had a twinge in my chest when I put the bags down. It took a second to pass. When you live with a damaged heart, all you can do is wait and see if *this* twinge is the big one.

"Are you all right?" she asked.

"Just a muscle spasm. Have you been crying?"

"Yes, I pulled over and lost it for a couple of minutes. The prosecution is killing us in court. The only people Josie Fletcher told about the abuse she endured were close friends. I don't think the jury is buying their stories."

"I'm sorry to hear that, Jen. I know how hard you've worked on this case and I know it's caused you a lot of personal agony." She opened the door leading into the kitchen from the garage.

"Yes, and I'm way too emotionally involved. I'm afraid it's affecting my judgment."

"I doubt that. I'd want you on my team if I were in her place."

"That's sweet of you, Shiloh, but we both know where good intentions can take us. How was your trip?"

"As well as any trip can go that starts and ends on an airplane," I answered.

"Did you find what you were looking for?" She began to make coffee.

"I found a piece of a puzzle that may come in handy, but we have suspects aplenty now where we had none before. And Robert Svenson, our only witness, was killed in Marietta last night. As soon as I shower and repack, I'm driving to Georgia again to see what I can find out."

"Do you think you're up to all this travel?" Jennifer asked. "Can't one of your detectives handle it?"

"Either of them could, but it's *my* case now."

"It was *their* case for two years, Lieutenant Tempest."

"You're right, but you know how I am. And to tell the truth, I'm feeling better than I've felt in years. I feel useful again."

"Just remember that a piece of equipment that requires an owner's manual is keeping your heartbeat regular and is all set to kick your heart if it starts to go bad.

"Oh well, get your shower and pack again and I'll fix us an omelet. You can at least take time to eat before you go."

FIFTEEN

Roy Johnson looked like an old-time movie cop. He was late forties or early fifties, was wearing a trench coat and a small gray Stetson hat, with a face that had twenty-four hours of stubble. "I'm glad you made it in, Lieutenant. Have a seat in the squad room and I'll get us a cup of coffee."

The squad room he had pointed out looked pretty much like the one back in Knoxville, only with fewer desks. I found the one with a name plate that said *Sgt. Roy Johnson* and took a seat beside it. Johnson's accent was distinctly Georgia to my ears.

There were Polaroid pictures on his desk that appeared to be from a crime scene. I resisted picking them up and was glad I did. Johnson hadn't gone far for the coffee. "I forgot to ask how you wanted it, so I bought a packet of creamer and sugar."

He put two Styrofoam cups of steaming coffee on the desk. "When did you get in, Lieutenant?"

"Yesterday evening around five. I waited until this morning because I figured you'd be on the move all night." I shook the sugar into my coffee and stirred it, cop style, with a ballpoint pen since there were no utensils handy.

"I *was* on the move most of the night. I slept about three hours this morning." He took a swig of coffee. "I spoke to the victim's mother after she flew in yesterday.

"She says her son was a witness to a murder a couple of years ago. He called her day before yesterday and told her he wouldn't be in his apartment for a while. She thinks he saw somebody or something that scared him."

"He left a message for me that same day, but I was out of town. I called when I got back, and you answered the phone, Sergeant."

"Svenson had packed a bag, but he never left his apartment. His stuff had been rummaged through and we think his laptop is missing. Lieutenant, could this murder he was witness to have been mob connected?"

"It's highly unlikely. Why do you ask?"

"Because Svenson was killed with a silenced Colt .22 semiautomatic pistol, and you can't pick up that kind of equipment at a flea market." Johnson took another swig of coffee, letting what he had just said sink in.

"How do you know what he was killed with?" I asked.

Johnson pushed the Polaroids on his desk towards me. One showed Robert Svenson on his back, eyes wide-open. The other was a close-up of a semiautomatic pistol.

"The shooter tossed the pistol on the bed when he was finished — after he put four rounds in the boy's chest and two in his head. He left no prints behind and didn't pick up the casings. He completely broke his connection to the murder scene.

"ATF picked it up this morning to see if they can run a trace. The silencer was homemade but it was made by somebody who knew what he was doing. This looks like a professional hit," Johnson said.

"Johnson, this has to remain confidential, but of our two chief suspects, one was Naval Intelligence and the other was a career Marine."

"Either of whom might have had the knowledge and skill to do this. Very interesting, Lieutenant. I wish he had stayed in your jurisdiction. We got zip to go on. The canvas turned up nothin' so far."

"Did Svenson open the door to his killer?"

"We don't know if he opened the door because somebody knocked or if he was on his way out and the shooter just caught him as he opened the door. If he was as scared as his mother says he was, it seems unlikely he'd answer the door without looking first."

"Fill me in on the murder you're investigating," Johnson said. "Svenson's mother was in no condition to elaborate after she identified her son's body."

"Robert had a female roommate. She was stabbed and died from the wounds. He opened his bedroom door and ran into the killer, who severely stabbed him with the same weapon. She was stabbed two dozen times and he was stabbed in several places with the same knife."

"Was he ever a suspect?"

"In the beginning he was, even with his severe wounds. We thought maybe it was a love affair gone bad, but DNA put the knife in another man's hand.

We think maybe Robert knew him and was too scared to speak up. I warned him that we were stirring the pot when I talked to him last week."

"This really doesn't seem like the same killer, Lieutenant — a passion killing and a cold-blooded assassination. I'm thinking Svenson was into something illegal and crossed the wrong person."

"It's a possibility, but I don't put a lot of stock in coincidences."

"Well, you know the drill, Lieutenant. I'll investigate where the leads take me. I'll keep you updated and you keep me updated."

"I appreciate it, Sergeant. Maybe between the two, of us we'll solve both our cases."

"You look tired, Loo," Reagan said. "You must have been here awhile."

"Yeah, I rode around with the detective in Marietta, looking at the crime scene and interviewing Svenson's associates at the electronics store. It was late last night when we finished, so I decided to just drive back."

"Did you get anything from his fellow workers?"

"No. Whatever scared him, it happened *after* work the day he called here. Everyone agreed he was acting normal until his shift ended."

"Did you turn anything on Quinn's whereabouts yesterday?"

"Yeah, I called the real estate firm he owns and pretended to be a customer. His secretary said he was in Birmingham, Alabama, and had been there a couple of days."

"That would have taken him close to Marietta. He could have stopped off and done the job on his way to Birmingham. The time frame fits."

"Yeah, or David Gettlefinger could have driven down and done it," Reagan said.

"You're right, Al. Either could have done it. Robert Svenson was killed with a silenced Colt .22."

"No kidding? I don't think I ever knew a murder cop who actually had a case where a silencer was used. That's mostly movie stuff."

"Quinn knew I had talked to Svenson and where he was because the Sheriff told him. How would Gettlefinger have known?"

"Loo, we shouldn't underestimate Gettlefinger. After you left yesterday, Culvahouse came by. It seems that Gettlefinger has been selling videos to an online voyeur site. He's computer savvy and you can log into any number of databases and track people by their Social Security numbers. He could have put two and two together after we raided his place yesterday. It would have been logical for him to go after Svenson."

"If we can prove the online sales, there's an enhanced punishment for making the videos," I said. "Not that it will help Robert Svenson. If he had just talked to me…"

"You can't beat yourself up for that, Loo. Svenson could have ended this any time by telling us who butchered Cynthia Quinn."

"Yeah, I know, but as much murder and mayhem as I've seen, I never get used to the utter waste. I'm going up to see if the Sheriff's here yet. If Freed brings biscuits, save me one."

"Will do," Reagan said.

As I started down the hall, I met Chief Tim Rosenbaum. "Excuse me, Lieutenant Tempest. I need a word with you."

"What happened to first names, Chief?"

"I just saw the request for your out-of-town trip to Georgia. You just got back from there a few days ago. You need to consolidate your trips. The expense comes out of *my* budget and I have to explain it when I go over!"

"Sorry, Chief, but murders don't happen on schedule."

"You've always thought you were above the rules, Lieutenant."

"No, Chief. I just don't have the rule book stuck up my ass."

He said something else as I walked away, but I didn't hear what it was. I took the center elevators up to the sheriff's department main offices.

"Good morning, Madeline. Is the Sheriff in?"

"Sheriff," Madeline said into an intercom, "Lieutenant Tempest is here."

"Send him in," Sam's voice crackled over the box."

I opened the door and went in. Sam was drinking coffee from a blue mug that said *Sam Renfro for Sheriff.*

"I see you got your intercom working, Sam."

"Yeah, I did. I got tired of Madeline knocking on the door. My predecessor liked seeing people go to a lot of trouble on his behalf. I don't."

96

"You have any more, Sam?"

"Always, Hoss." He turned around and poured coffee from a pot on the table behind him into a cup like the one he was drinking from. "One sugar, right, Shiloh?"

"You have a good memory, Sam."

"We spent a lot of time on stakeouts in our day." He handed me the coffee from across his desk. "Do I need to get out my ashtray for this talk?"

"Not unless you just want a free smoke."

"What the hell." He got the metal ashtray and butane lighter out. "Give me one of your Camels."

We both lit up and sat sipping coffee for a minute or so, just like the old days when we worked patrol and later narcotics.

"So what was the trip to Atlanta about this time?" Sam finally asked.

"How did you know about the trip? I just got back."

"Chief Rosenbaum was waiting when I came in to complain about how you're ruining his budget by taking unnecessary trips. If he wasn't so connected, I'd have his ass sitting in a pod at the jail, guarding prisoners."

"Our only witness to Cynthia Quinn's murder got popped in Marietta with a silenced Colt .22, semiautomatic."

"No shit? In twenty-eight years I never had a case involving a genuine assassin's weapon. I take it you think the killing is connected to your investigation?" Sam said.

"The detective in Marietta thinks Svenson was mixed up in something dirty and got in over his head. I think it's too much of a coincidence that Svenson got killed just days after I interviewed him. He tried to call me and told his mother he was leaving his apartment for a few days. He almost made it. The killer got him at the door with his bags packed."

"Who outside this department knew where he was?" Sam asked, taking a sip of coffee and putting out his cigarette.

"Well, Quinn knew because you told him right before our little incident."

"Oh hell, Shiloh! I *did* tell him — and told him what kind of work he was doing. I might as well have drawn him a map. I'm losing my touch."

"No, you were just trying to pacify a citizen because that's your job. It didn't ring a bell with me until I found out what had happened to Robert Svenson. And Quinn isn't the only suspect we're working now."

"David Gettlefinger?"

"Yeah, and he's a lot smarter than I thought he was. He's been selling videos he makes to an online voyeur site, and Reagan pointed out that any computer savvy person can track down almost anyone. And Gettlefinger was on the loose during the killing. He's an ex-Marine with skills and maybe the contacts to get hold of a silencer — or even make one."

"By the way," Sam opened a desk drawer and took out a fat manila envelope, "here's the stuff you asked for, including a copy of the video of the fracas."

"Thanks, Sam. I hope there's nothing here I can use."

"Well, Hoss, I have to go to a budget meeting with county commission. You going to be around for lunch? We could go out to Litton's for a juicy cheeseburger and Key lime pie."

"No, I'm running on fumes. I've been up twenty-four hours and I'm going home and get some sleep."

"Give Jen my best?"

"Thanks, Sam. I'll do that.

SIXTEEN

Once when I lived in Charlotte, North Carolina, two apartments down from mine there was a family with a mentally challenged son of thirty or so, who had only one album by Roger Miller, the one with *King of the Road* and *Dang Me*. There were other songs but those were the two I remember

Phillip --that was his name-- had a record player and the album was his greatest treasure. Every warm sunny day, he would open the window, in the days before almost every place was air conditioned, and play that album over and over again. He would clap his hands as he had watched other people do but he had no rhythm at all.

I awoke from a dream of those days in my bed at Jennifer's house, hearing Phillip's Roger Miller album, but it wasn't the dream state music that woke me. It was the soft sobbing coming from across the hall. I had gone to bed at one o'clock in the afternoon and it was now dark. I rolled over and looked at my watch and saw that it was nearly ten.

Moving as quietly as I could, I made my way in the dark to Jennifer's room. She had her face buried in the pillow to muffle her sobs but her body was shaking.

"Jen, what's wrong?" I asked

She raised her head and turned to look at me. In the light filtering through the window, I could see that her face was wet.

"Shiloh, I'm sorry I woke you. I was very quite while I was showering and getting ready for bed." She sniffed quietly.

"What's wrong, Jen?" I sat on the side of her bed.

"Josie Fletcher was found guilty of second degree murder. I *failed* her, Shiloh. She trusted me and I failed her!" Her body began to shake again.

I lifted the sheet and slipped under it, taking Jennifer in my arms. She molded her trembling body to mine, tears wetting my shoulder and neck as I held her tightly in my arms.

"You didn't fail her, Jen. You did the best you could. Nobody knows what a jury will do, or why. You did your best. That's all anyone can do."

"I know that, Shiloh. But she looked so defeated and confused as the court officers took her away. She's so alone, and *I* felt so alone. Hold me tighter."

With the faint odor of orange blossoms in nostrils and her hair tickling my face and her soft breasts touching my bare chest through the light gown, I felt a stirring that had been gone for a long time. Jen felt it too. She searched for my face in the dark and began to kiss me voraciously — and I responded.

Then Jennifer pushed away and I was confused for an instant until I heard her nightgown tear as she pulled it over her head. Then her bare breasts were against my chest and I could feel her nipples become erect. She was tugging at my shorts and I raised my hips so she could pull them away. She raised up in the bed and jerked them the rest of the way off.

Her long mane of hair was falling across her breasts for a moment in the moonlit room, then her mouth was on mine again and it was as if she were sucking energy from the core of my being. She rolled over on her back, pulling me with her and spread her legs. I slid between them and was inside her before I realized it.

"Oh yes, Shiloh. Oh *yes!*"

It was brief and fierce, our first real love-making in two years. She locked her legs around me and we rocked from side to side until both of us felt ourselves rising to a peak that had seemed out of reach forever.

When the emptying out, the total lack of control that is orgasm, sent us into spasms, I knew I was healed from years of frustration. We stayed locked together for perhaps a minute, until I finally withdrew and rolled onto my back, taking a deep breath.

"If *that* didn't set off your defibrillator, Lieutenant Tempest, I think it will hold up through almost anything." She laughed and rolled over on her stomach to look at me.

"Your mascara's a wreck, Counselor," I said, moving nervously.

"It's all right," she said. "Light up. You always do afterwards."

"I'll have to go to my room."

"No, the ashtray and lighter are in the same drawer where you always kept them. I replaced the pack you left with a fresh pack when you came back to visit."

I sat up on the side of the bed and turned on the bedside lamp. The ashtray, lighter and cigarettes were there. I lit one and inhaled deeply. Jen was on her elbow watching, a smile on her face.

"I figured you would have cleaned out this nightstand long ago. You always hated it when I smoked."

"I hated it worse when you weren't here to smoke," she said.

"Jen, I'm sorry for what I put you through. I don't know why it happened."

"We won't analyze it, Shiloh. Let's just say that you're a complex man and *all* the parts have to be working for you function at full capacity — mind, spirit and body. You got locked into yourself, somehow. Now you've escaped."

"That's a good description, Jen."

"I know it is. I'm a brilliant trial lawyer with a double major in psychology and sociology." She laughed again and it reminded me of why I had fallen in love with her in the first place. Why she fell in love with me, I'll probably never understand.

"How did Josie Fletcher take the verdict?" I asked.

Jennifer's face clouded over for a moment. "The same way anybody would feel looking at a possible twenty-five years. But I've already filed notice of appeal."

"Of course you have. And you'll win it, too."

"Do you know what I'd like to do, Shiloh?"

"I'll have to rest awhile first," I said.

"Maybe *that* later. I'd like to go the Waffle House for an omelet full of jalapenos and cheese, like we used to do."

"That, I can manage, Jen."

She laughed again and it was like music.

The video of my skirmish with Joshua Quinn flickered on the portable CD player. There was no sound but I watched it several times from the point where Quinn came around the table until he went out on Rosenbaum's shoulder. I was still watching it when Freed came through the door.

"Golly, Lieutenant, you're here early," he said putting down a bag of biscuits on his desk.

"John, has anyone ever told you that you *look* like Ron Howard when he played Opie on the *Andy Griffin Show* and *sound* like Ron Howard when he played Richie Cunningham on *Happy Days?*"

"Heck, yeah, Loo. Opie was my nickname for years. I brought bacon, cheese and egg biscuits this morning. I see you have the coffee ready. I saw Al go into the restroom, so he'll be here in a minute."

"And you don't mind being called Opie or known as the *least* profane cop I've ever heard talk?"

"Nope. I am who I am, Loo, and I ain't nothing else."

"Here's a twenty dollar bill, John. If you're going to bring the daily cholesterol, I'm going to pay my share."

"If that's what you want to do, Shiloh, it tickles me to death." He took the money and stuck it in his shirt pocket.

"John, some time today would you dig out the surveillance video from the drugstore you told me about the first day I was here?"

"Sure, Loo. But it's pretty low quality."

"That's all right, John. I just want to look at it."

"Good morning, John; good morning, Shiloh," Reagan rumbled as he came through the door. "How are the two of you today?"

"I'm good," Freed said.

"I'm fantastic, Al. Just fantastic."

"Somebody feed you a happy pill, Loo?" Reagan asked, going back to pour himself a cup of coffee.

"Something like that, Al," I said.

"I could get used to having a supervisor fix my coffee every morning," Reagan said. "With John bringing in food and you making coffee, I don't even really need a wife."

"Sure you do," Freed said. "Somebody has to keep you from wearing stripes and plaid together. Besides, neither of us wants you trying to snuggle with us." Freed reached over and rubbed Reagan's prickly hair as the big detective reached into the bag to get a biscuit. "You just ain't soft enough, Al."

"Leave me a biscuit," I said, fishing out a report from the clutter on my desk. "There's something I need to check while I'm thinking of it," I told them. "Be back shortly."

My destination was one floor up and a short walk past the jail visitation area. The officer in the sallyport, which is what you call the entrance and exit to a jail, stared at me curiously as I went by. The sallyport is where rookies and old men waiting for retirement usually work. The one on duty was the first variety and I didn't know him.

The evidence room is actually a bank vault. I walked up to the counter of the half-door and looked in. I saw a young man in a class A uniform and decided he was fresh from the academy. Class B uniforms are authorized for personnel working inside. They're more comfortable but a rookie can't wear a shiny new badge in class Bs.

To avoid being questioned, I produced my badge. "I'm Lieutenant Tempest. I was wondering if you could help me out."

"If I can, Lieutenant," he said, walking to the counter.

"Would you still have a hard copy of a receipt to release a piece of evidence from two years ago."

"S?re, we keep copies for five years. What is it?"

I handed him the report and he walked out of sight. I could hear a filing cabinet open and paper shuffling, then he called out loud enough for me to hear him: "Lieutenant, I found it! Do you want me to burn you a copy?"

"If you don't mind."

A couple of minutes later, he handed me the original report I had given him and a copy of the corresponding receipt for release of property.

"Who usually signs off on evidence release?" I asked, looking at the name beside Cynthia Quinn's name on the receipt for the purse that had been taken from her car when it was burglarized and later turned in.

"Usually the officer who logged it in, but sometimes a supervisor comes with the victim and signs the release."

"Thanks, Officer," I said, walking away while studying the receipt.

SEVENTEEN

As soon as I walked back into the office I knew something had excited the two detectives. When John Freed spoke, I knew for sure because the pitch of his voice had risen beyond its near-contralto pitch.

"Look, we just got a call from Gettlefinger's cousin, the one he took the car from. He says he went by an old house Gettlefinger's been fixing up out off Andersonville Pike and the car's hidden under some brush behind the house."

"You two ready to go get him?" I asked.

"Maybe we should send patrol or even the SWAT team," Reagan said, glancing away from me, then shooting a look at Freed.

"Did the Sheriff tell you to take care of the old man?" I asked.

"Something like that, Loo. After you had to go in for the last surgery," Freed said.

"Well, I guess you'll have to tell the Sheriff I gave you a direct order and he wasn't here to intervene."

"No doubt, we'd *have* to obey a direct order, Loo," Reagan grinned.

"Then let's hit the garage and get our vests and a couple of shotguns. I've never been much for letting someone else do my dirty work. I'm parked on L-5."

We locked up the office and headed for the elevators. As we passed the major crime unit squad room, Tim Rosenbaum called out to us. We stopped. "Let me handle this," I said under my breath.

"Where are the three of you going this time of morning?"

"We have a lead to run down," I said.

"And it takes all three of you to run down a lead?" He scowled. "I doubt that."

"Well, since it's *my* squad and *my* call, Chief, we'll see you when we get back." Reagan and Freed were both smiling.

"You two detectives enjoy your insubordination while you can," Rosenbaum said. "When Tempest is gone and you're *mine* again, we'll see how you do working general assignment and doing vandalism reports!"

"Later, Chief," I said.

"You have time sheets due today, Tempest!" Rosenbaum yelled at our retreating backs.

"He's so anal," Reagan said when we were out of earshot. "I bet the vegetables in his kitchen cabinets are in alphabetical order."

"That's probably why his third wife has left him," Freed said.

"You don't have any room to talk there," Reagan said.

"My women leave because I'm too much of a sex machine. His leave because he can't get it up, I've heard."

"Where did you hear about his last marriage breaking up?" I asked.

"A couple of guys in general assignment heard him talking to her on the phone. They said he was almost crying, trying to get her to come home," Freed replied.

"Where did you hear the other thing?" I asked as we got on the elevator to the parking garage.

"My last wife knew his second wife. They worked together. She used to always complain that Rosenbaum couldn't perform unless he tied her up or put handcuffs on her. He made her pretend she was *scared*, to get him excited. Now that's kinky," Freed said, as the elevator lurched downward.

"Maybe that's what happens when a man's wives keep getting younger and younger," Reagan said as the elevator came to a stop and the doors opened on L-4. "Eventually, he *can't* keep up. I get off here. I'll drive down and meet you two on L-5."

By the time Reagan caught up with us, we had loaded Freed's vest and Mossberg pump shotgun in my car. The big burr-headed detective got out and removed his vest and shotgun from the trunk of his car and put them in my trunk.

"How long's it been since you had this much adrenaline pumping, Loo?"

"Too long, Reagan, too long. Let's roll."

It was a thirty minute ride out to Andersonville Pike and it took a few minutes to locate the old house on Pleasant Gap Road. We had grown quiet the last few miles, preparing ourselves mentally. Nobody is ever entirely prepared.

"There's the house, Loo," Reagan said. It was an old stone house that probably dated from before World War II or earlier, but the doors and window seemed to be later additions.

I drove by slowly enough to get a good look, but not slowly enough to draw Gettlefinger's attention if he happened to be looking out the window. "I saw the sun glint off the car under the brush pile, Loo," Freed whispered, though there was no reason to. "It was back to the left, near the woods."

"He's probably here, then," I said. "Freed, I'm going to drop you by the road, since you're the youngest and most athletic. Work your way through the woods and cover the back of the house in case he bolts. Reagan and I will make one more pass of the house and come in from the other direction, since there's no window in front on that side."

"Sounds good, Loo," Freed said as I pulled into the driveway of an abandoned barn.

Outside the car, we retrieved our Kevlar vests from the trunk and strapped them on without talking. As always before action, I felt my bladder twinge and wished I had emptied it before we started our trip. I knew the other two were experiencing the same thing, but nobody mentioned it. Both detectives racked a round into their Mossberg pumps and checked the safety, and we all checked our Glocks and extra magazines.

"Call it in, Reagan," I said. "Get patrol on the way for transport. Tell them to hang back until we call for them."

The big detective took the portable from its leather case and keyed the mike. Nothing happened. He moved a few feet away and tried it again with the same result.

"We're in a dead spot, Loo," Reagan said.

"How can there be a dead spot in a multimillion dollar radio system that's been online since before I left the department?"

"There ain't many, Loo," Freed said. "But this is apparently one of them."

"All right, then, gentleman. Shall we fall back and let patrol do it?"

"And let them have all the glory, Loo?" Reagan said. "We're already here, so I say let's take the slimy bastard down."

"Freed?"

"I agree with Reagan, Loo. Let's do it."

"So be it," I said, my stomach knotting up.

We got back into the compact Chevrolet and drove slowly up the road. I stopped and let Freed out. He walked into the woods without further comment, and we drove by the house one more time.

"Any sign of movement?" I asked.

"No, it looks the same as before."

A hundred feet up the road, I pulled the car onto the shoulder, off the road as far as I could, and we walked back down the winding asphalt road until we were at the edge of the overgrown yard. "I'm going to move into position beside the door. The walls are too thick for him to shoot through them."

"There's Freed. He's in position, Loo. Back behind the brush pile. He's using the car for cover."

"All right, then. Start moving down that ditch until you're directly in front of the house and I'll go to the porch. Put your hand up when you're in position and stay low."

He nodded, dropped into a crouch and duck-walked. The yard was elevated above the road, so Reagan had good cover. When he was almost there, I sprinted up into the yard, angling towards the front porch.

By the time I got to the porch, my breath was ragged and I thought of what Jennifer had said last night. Hopefully she was right. My heart was pounding, but I was totally alert and alive. A plank in the wooden porch creaked as I stepped up and flattened myself against the rough stone. Reagan raised his hand and pulled it down quickly to show he was in position.

I edged to the wooden door, reached out and hit it with my fist, three times, then quickly withdrew it. "Gettlefinger, you're surrounded, Come out with your hands up!"

There was movement inside the house and a moment later, splinters began to fly as rounds tore through the wooden door. From the sound of the shots, I had no doubt it was the 1911 Model .45. The shooting stopped for a second and I heard an empty magazine hit the floor inside, just before Reagan shot the window out with his shotgun. My ears were ringing and it seemed to grow louder as a momentary silence followed.

"Gettlefinger, we don't want to kill you. Let's talk!" I yelled.

Something turned over inside the house — a chair perhaps — and footsteps thudded through the small house. I heard the back door open, then Freed yelled: "Police! Don't move!"

The back door slammed shut again and footsteps once more thudded across the floor. I braced myself, but the shots I expected were not fired. *Dear God,* I found myself praying silently, *I don't want to die now and I don't want to kill this man.* It had been a long time since I prayed.

"Gettlefinger, let's talk! Nobody has been hurt so far! You have nowhere to go."

"I didn't kill that girl and I ain't goin' to prison for it." His voice was verging on hysterical, but the sound came clearly through the shattered window.

"*That's* not why we're here," I yelled, holding my pistol at the ready, just in case he came out shooting. "We have a warrant on you for the videos you made of the women at the apartments."

"The *videos?* How did you know about the videos?" He sounded genuinely surprised.

"Shelia Andrews in 27-A found your camera while she was cleaning the bathroom and called us," I yelled. "It's against the law to videotape people when they don't know about it. She signed a warrant. That's *all* it is, David."

"I'm *not* a murder suspect?"

"No, all we have on you is the warrant for the video," I yelled. And it was technically true.

He was quiet for thirty seconds or so. "What will they do to me for the videos?"

"It's a Mickey Mouse charge, David. You're a decorated Marine. A good lawyer will get you off with probation."

"How come you brought so many guys when you came to the apartments?" He sounded a lot calmer.

"We knew there was one camera, but we thought there might be more. We brought enough officers for a search. Now we know there was only the one camera."

I took a deep breath and gave him a while to think about it.

"No jail time for the videos? Are you sure?" He was wavering and I could tell he *wanted* to believe me.

"I can guarantee that you won't do any time for *making* the videos, David." *Though it's possible having sold them online might mandate some time,* I thought.

"How do I come outta here without bein' shot?" he asked.

"Put your pistol out the window and drop it. Be careful not to cut your self on the glass. Then open the door and come out with your fingers laced behind your head. Move slowly and I promise you won't get hurt."

His arm came gingerly through the window and the pistol thudded on the wooden porch. "I'm coming out like you said."

The door opened and he came out slowly with his fingers laced behind his head. He had several days' growth of blond beard on his face and was apparently wearing what he had fled the apartment complex in. It was unlikely he had been to Georgia.

"Stop right there. I have a pistol pointed at you. There's an officer going to come out of the ditch in front of the house. When he gets you cuffed, I'll stop pointing my weapon at you."

Reagan came out of the ditch, huffing and puffing, and made his way across the front yard, shotgun held at port arms. Three minutes later, Gettlefinger was wearing cuffs. I stepped to the side of the house and yelled for Freed, and he came around the house thirty seconds later.

"Freed, take the car up to Andersonville Pike and call for transport."

"Loo," Reagan said. "You're face is bleeding."

I reached up and found a sliver of wood protruding from the skin, just below my left eye. I pulled it out and a little more blood flowed freely down my face.

"It's just a flesh wound," I said like a movie cop. Suddenly the three of us were laughing from the relief of being alive and in one piece.

"Are ya'll crazy?" Gettlefinger asked, which set us off again.

We had stopped laughing by the time Freed called in our situation from up on Andersonville Pike and three patrol units showed up, followed five minutes later by a news crew. They were videotaping the splintered door and shattered window when we left. I told them to get a statement from the patrol supervisor.

Jennifer was waiting when I got home. "I saw you on the news and you were bleeding."

"As you can see, it was just a splinter of wood where David Gettlefinger shot through the front door," I replied.

She looked closely at my face. The nurse from down in the jail had cleaned it and applied a liquid bandage. She put her arms around me. "Tempest, are you familiar with the term *patrol officers,* as in husky young men with good reflexes and healthy hearts?"

"That's what Sheriff Sam told me when we were booking Gettlefinger, but he was as proud of me as you are. Jen, my love, I haven't been so *alive* in years. I'm still tingling all over. Today was just a bonus after last night. I even said a prayer today. I don't know if it counts because I was so scared, but I did it."

"It counts," she said. "Come on to the dining room. I took the afternoon off and slaved over a gourmet meal."

I put my arm around her waist and we walked to the dining room. "Smells like food from the Mandarin House buffet," I said.

"Okay, so I cheated a little. I stuck it in the microwave to reheat when you pulled into the driveway. I got you General Tso's chicken and hot and sour soup, and I got myself sweet and sour chicken and egg drop soup. And I got both of us a box of steamed rice."

"Did you get egg rolls and crab Rangoon dumplings?"

"Of course. And plenty of duck sauce and mustard. When I prepare takeout food, I go all the way. Have a seat and I'll serve."

In a few minutes we were putting away Chinese food and it was as if I hadn't tasted anything for years before that moment. I took a spoonful of hot and sour soup, not only savoring the taste but also the texture.

"I know you had and interesting day," Jen said, "and so did I. It didn't entail as much adrenalin as yours, but to me it's big." I looked at her and saw the miraculous woman I had tried to walk away from.

"What?" she asked. "What are you thinking?"

"I'm just enjoying dinner with my beautiful, intelligent, Latina beauty."

"You're not going to try and make up for two years of sex in a week, are you?"

"No, I'm not. Tell me what happened today, Jen."

"I was contacted by Josie Fletcher's sister-in-law, her dead husband's sister. She verified that Josie's husband was a monster. I won't know the details until I meet with her in Indianapolis next week, but she hinted at perversions and sadism on his part."

"Why didn't she come forward?" I asked.

"She did. As a matter of fact, she says she called Adam Linkous, the assistant attorney general who prosecuted Josie, and gave him the story."

"Linkous withheld exculpatory evidence in a murder case? "

"It appears so. I'm going to Indianapolis to get her sworn statement and take it to the trial judge. If I'm lucky, Josie will get out on bond pending a new trial, and Linkous will lose his law license. And the last couple of days — I got *real* lucky, as you know." She lowered her eyelids in a mock sensual manner and stared at me.

"I know that better than anyone, Jen."

"All right, Lieutenant, tell me about your adventure today," she said.

"All right. Once upon a time, there was a man named David Gettlefinger who wanted to be a filmmaker..."

EIGHTEEN

"Gettlefinger today, Loo? It's just you and me. Freed's gone to the dentist. He cracked a molar on a pearl from a can of oyster stew." Al Reagan had just come in and put his briefcase on the table.

"So we won't have any biscuits today? How can I function without my morning biscuits? Al, I've grown used to a certain standard."

"That's why I stopped and picked them up myself — sausage, egg and cheese." Reagan opened his briefcase, which was laid out as neatly as a military footlocker, and removed the two biscuits. "Be my guest, Loo."

Reagan poured himself a cup of coffee and we sat in a comradely silence eating our biscuits and sipping coffee for a few minutes.

"You say Freed broke a molar on a pearl from a can of oyster stew? That's what I'd call ironic," I said.

"Yep, Shiloh, it is ironic, but my little buddy Freed will probably have the pearl made into a tie tack or something. If you pelt him with lemons, he always comes back with lemonade. He's a hard man to keep down."

"He is a cheerful man," I said. "Maybe he marries women who can't stand *that.*"

"Have you heard from Chief Rosenbaum this morning?" Reagan asked, knocking biscuit crumbs off his shirt and tie.

"Not directly. He went to the Sheriff yesterday afternoon, before we even got back, to file for disciplinary action for my insubordinate behavior and for failing to call for backup."

"What did the Sheriff do?"

"Told Rosenbaum he'd think it over, then ran the request through the shredder," I said, taking my last bite of biscuit, cheese and sausage.

"You never did answer my question, Loo. We gonna take a run on Gettlefinger this morning?"

"Even as we speak, the jail is taking him to the interrogation room."

"What if I'd been late today?"

"You're *never* late, Al. You walk through that door at exactly 0750 every morning, and Freed usually follows by two or three minutes. So I knew we'd have our biscuits and coffee in time to interview Gettlefinger at 0805."

"Am I that predictable, Shiloh?"

"We all are, Al. You just have to pay attention. Let's lock up our weapons and go talk to Gettlefinger. He's been stewing all night so we need to stir the pot."

It was a short walk to the interrogation room. A muscled jailer with a shaved head waited outside the door. I didn't know if he was the same guard as the last time because so many officers these days look like weightlifters with shaved heads. We could see Gettlefinger in leg irons and handcuffs attached to the table.

We went in and pulled up two chairs from against the wall and sat directly across from him. He had shaved since the day before and was wearing a clean jail-issue orange jumpsuit. Reagan picked up a Miranda release from the stack on the table and pushed it in front of Gettlefinger.

"Read this and sign it," Reagan said.

"I ain't sign' nothin'," He said.

"All right," I told him. "We'll tell the jailer to lock you back up and you can discuss the particulars of your case with a public defender for about two minutes before your arraignment and bail hearing. It will be a lawyer who has a hundred other cases. But *we* don't have a conversation and any chance of helping yourself goes down the tube the minute we walk out of here."

"All right. I'll read it and sign it," he said. He took it, glanced over it and signed his name. Reagan looked at it and nodded his head.

"All right, Gettlefinger, let's talk," I told him.

"Lieutenant Tempest, you told me yesterday that the only thing you had on me was makin' them videos. The jailers told me I'm charged with two counts of attempted first degree murder and interstate traffickin' in child pornography."

"The warrant *was* for the illegal videos. But that was before you tried to kill two police officers," I said.

"What about the child pornography? I ain't ever been into children."

"There were at least three naked kids on videos we've looked at so far," Reagan told him. "That enhances the charge of selling pornography over the internet and allowed us to get a much bigger bond. All told, your bond is four hundred thousand dollars. And men in jail for sex crimes involving children don't fare well."

"The kids just *happened* to be in the videos. I was recordin' their mothers naked, not them," Gettlefinger said.

"That's what *we* think, David. And if you cooperate with us, the part about child pornography might go away — so that you don't have to be segregated in a cell alone the entire time you're in jail," I told him. "And you *are* going to jail. We're just establishing how long it might be and where you might serve it."

"I didn't hurt anybody. I'm a good man."

"You took advantage of women, you put their most private moments on the internet and you fired eight rounds at the two of us! Is that how a good man behaves?" Reagan asked.

"Just tell me how I can cooperate. I'm ashamed, whether you believe it or not." He dropped his head and stared at the table.

"David, you can start by telling us where your Colt .22 semiautomatic pistol is. It wasn't in your truck, your apartment or the house where you were staying. Where is it?"

"I ain't got a Colt pistol!"

"Aw, geez, Lieutenant, the first words out of his mouth and he's lying. Let's send this scumbag back downstairs and go play a round of golf," Reagan said.

"Let's give him a chance, Detective. David, we found receipts from the target range in your apartment — the range off Lovell Road. You fired that pistol there and you bought ammo there. And the guy who manages the place confirmed that you shot a Colt .22"

"I *had* one, but I sold it three months ago at a gun show on Clinton Highway," Gettlefinger said.

"Now how convenient is *that*? You probably don't know the guy you sold it to because it was a cash transaction, right?" Reagan asked.

"That's right," Gettlefinger said, "but I sold it for four hundred dollars and I bought a new camera the same day for just over four hundred. I'd had the pistol a long time and I hated to sell it, but I wanted a better camera."

"So there'll be a receipt for a four hundred dollar camera you bought sometime in February in one of those shoe boxes you use for filing cabinets?" I said.

"I swear to God, it's true, Lieutenant!"

"Tell us where you were for the two days after you ran away from the apartment complex," I said. "And don't lie to me. I have an eyewitness that puts you and that car in Marietta, Georgia, during that time period." The question was a bluff, but I wanted a reaction.

"Lieutenant, I had to *push* that car the last hundred yards to get it into the field where you found it. I ran out of gas in front of the house the same day I borrowed it from my cousin because I was afraid to stop for gas. A guy named Bill Clement, who lives at the top of the hill east of my house, helped me push it where it was," Gettlefinger said.

"You know it's only going to take us a little while to check these things out, don't you?" I said.

"Sure, I know that, but I ain't worried because they're *true*," he said. And I knew he was telling the truth.

"Well, we're going to check your story and get back with you," I said.

"Aintcha gonna ask me about the videos?" Gettlefinger asked.

"We don't need to ask you about them," Reagan said. "They speak for themselves."

"What about the child porn charge, Lieutenant?"

"If you've told us the truth, I'll go see the assistant district attorney about removing the child porn charge, but you're going down for the rest of it," I said.

And for a man looking at the possibility of prison, Gettlefinger looked relieved. Even people outside the system know what happens to child molesters in prison. Everyone watches television.

"Oh, by the way, we need a sample of your DNA. Will I need a court order?" I asked.

"No, sir," Gettlefinger said.

"Good. I'll have someone from forensics come by and collect it."

We stepped outside and told the jailer to take Gettlefinger back to his cell, then started back to our office.

"You believe him, don't you, Loo?"

"Yeah, I believe him. But we'll wait on the DNA."

"Wouldn't it be nice if DNA really worked the way it does on television and in the movies? Collect a sample and identify it before the shift ends," Reagan said.

"Yes, it would. I called the lab yesterday to check on Quinn's DNA. I thought the technician I talked to was going to laugh right in my face. We may get it back in three weeks, but a month or more is more like it."

"So where do we go from here, Lou?"

"I think tomorrow we'll see if we can talk to Emma Quinn while her husband's at work. You need to type up your notes from Chattanooga, if you haven't already done it."

"You mean like the name of the prostitute, the amount he paid her, and the name of the bellhop who set it up?" Reagan asked.

"We'll use what we need," I said.

Back in the office, I started a fresh pot of coffee.

"Loo, somebody has tampered with the lock on this filing cabinet — the one we put the dummy file in," Reagan said.

"How can you tell?"

"I wedged a little ball of paper behind it so that it would fall off if anyone moved it. Also, there's some fresh scratch marks on the bottom. Do you think Rosenbaum has the skill to open a padlock without prying it open?"

"When we were on patrol, he had a set of picks to open locked cars for citizens. I imagine he still has them. It's not a sophisticated lock."

Reagan opened the lock and looked into the cabinet. "Someone's definitely been in here, Loo. I had another paper wad wedged between the first two folders and it's in the bottom of the drawer."

"Al, why don't you talk to Culvahouse on the sly and see if he can install a lipstick cam somewhere in the office? It would be embarrassing, if nothing else, if we caught him on video breaking into a filing cabinet."

"Lieutenant, that's a perfectly evil plan."

"All's fair in love and war," I said. "Al, I'm going to take the rest of the day off."

"You're not sick are you, Shiloh?" Al looked concerned.

"No, as a matter of fact, I haven't felt better in years. The time cards Rosenbaum wants are on my desk. You can look through Gettlefinger's boxes, if you like. Look for that receipt, and check with the guy he says helped him push the car into the field, if you have time. Tomorrow we'll go see Emma Quinn, if we can catch her while her husband isn't around."

NINETEEN

Mike Bolander sat with his fingers laced across his stomach. Broad through the shoulders, thinning hair, he's a big man with a prizefighter's face. He looks more like a cop than a psychotherapist, maybe because he was a cop for ten years and a Golden Gloves champion before that. He had taught a course at the police academy and we had become friends.

"Let me be certain that I understand why you're here, Shiloh. The last time we talked, you were suffering from impotence and deep depression. You're here today because the impotence cleared up and you're all but euphoric. That right?"

"Hell no! I want to know what happened to me. *Why* am I functioning again and *why* do I feel so good? Or, I suppose I want to know how to hold on to it."

"Shiloh, for a man who understands human nature so well, you're remarkably dense when it comes to seeing yourself," Mike said.

"We're not going to descend into psychobabble, are we, Mike?"

"Shiloh, do you know what depression was once called?" He asked, ignoring my remark about his profession.

"No, I don't, Mike."

"It was called the *poet's melancholia*, because it afflicted so many writers. What they were describing was probably bipolar disorder, or as they used to say in my business, manic-depression."

"What's the difference?" I asked.

"Nobody is creative or fully functional during clinical depression. The poetry and the books were probably produced during manic states, when all seemed right with the world. It's a cycle we couldn't break until the last few decades."

"Are you trying to say I'm bipolar? I've seen manic people climbing the walls. That's never happened to me."

"Shiloh, not all manic states are extreme. You first saw the manic people when you were in the Army hospital, after you came back from Vietnam, correct?"

"Yeah, I guess that was the first time."

"What was it you did in Vietnam, Shiloh?"

"I was in the 173rd Light Infantry Brigade, a paratrooper, stationed at Dak Tho most of my time there."

"Where you were awarded the Bronze Star with a 'V" for Valor, for actions on Hill 875, one of the fiercest battles of the war. Is that correct?"

"How did you know… yes, that's correct."

"How did you feel while you were in a combat zone, Shiloh? Any depression?"

"I was scared to death. That's a silly question."

"It was after you got state-side that you had to be hospitalized. Is that correct?"

"Yeah, it was post traumatic stress. Happened to a lot of soldiers."

"During your career at the Sheriff's Department, did you ever get lost in depression or were you able to function all the time?" Mike took out a pack of Pall Malls and lit one.

"I had my ups and down."

"Yes, we all do. But you were a good cop. What made you feel best?"

"Well, when I was a little low, I'd jump a hot call and feel better," I said.

"By *hot call*, you mean a place where violence was happening or was apt to happen. Afterwards, you always felt better. Right?"

"That's what I just told you."

"Do you see a pattern, Shiloh? You thrive on action, then you crash when you don't have any. Did you suffer from depression before you went in the Army?"

"The first spell I remember, I was thirteen."

"Shiloh, your sexual function came back and the depression lifted within days of going back to work. I'd guess that something happened to get the adrenaline flowing the first few days, because the temptation would have been too much for you to pass up."

"Yeah, I had a violent encounter with a thug. Am I an adrenaline junkie?"

"Are you?" Mike took a deep drag and stared at me.

"You're the shrink," I said.

"Eventually you would have cycled back again, anyway — if you didn't kill yourself first. That's the nature of your disease, but your body gave you a big dose of nature's own antidepressant. What we try to duplicate with pills, but haven't been able to, you got for just risking your life."

"So in order to feel functional, I have to keep doing this job, which is hell on my heart and the rest of my body?"

"Shiloh, there will come a day when you realize how ludicrous it is to be hobbling to your police car. Nothing lasts forever. When that day comes, we can prescribe you medication to keep you from cycling in and out. I won't kid you; you'll never hit the highs again, but you'll be out of danger from eating your gun. Meanwhile, try to live in the moment."

"You realize, don't you, Mike, that I was hoping for a more metaphysical answer. You know, about my indomitable artist's spirit and intellectual strength."

"Shiloh, you're the dreamer. I'm a therapist. You're stuck in a human body with accompanying frailties, like everyone else. You'll have to sell your myths to the readers. Medications aren't romantic, but they work."

On the way home, pondering what Mike Bolander had said, I stopped at Ingle's supermarket and picked up two boneless, thick pork loin chops, stove top dressing, green beans, dinner rolls and a couple of sweet potatoes. I had decided to surprise Jennifer with a home-cooked meal. It had been awhile since I had cooked for the two of us.

It was a gorgeous day. Flowers were blooming everywhere, recovering from the freeze, and fluffy cotton-like clouds scudded across a sky the color of a blue topaz. On impulse, I pulled into a liquor store near the house and went in.

"Hey, Shiloh," the clerk said, "I haven't seen you in a while. Have you been away?"

"Yes, I have, Kenny. But I'm back."

"Working on a new book?"

"As a matter of fact, I'm going to start a new one today, I think. It will be about a washed-up novelist who gets back his groove."

"Sounds like a good idea. How can I help you, Shiloh?"

"I need a light, sweet dinner wine, Kenny."

"A Zinfandel, maybe? I have something I like --it's Russian River Zinfandel. It has a real berry taste to it and runs about thirty bucks."

"Bag it, then. I know your taste in wine is better than mine."

On the way home, I took a leisurely tour of the neighborhood, as if seeing it for the first time. The children were in school but adults were mowing and working in flower gardens. I pulled into our yard and noted that it needed mowing. The house itself, however, was in good shape.

I carried in the groceries and put the pork chops into the refrigerator. I found the ice bucket under the sink and was rinsing it out when the phone rang. I picked up and Al Reagan was on the line.

"Loo, sorry to bother you at home, but I got a call from Sergeant Roy Johnson from the Marietta Police Department. I didn't know if you wanted your home phone number given out, so I took his number and extension. He says he has info for you on the Robert Svenson case."

"Give me the number," I said, digging out my pen and reaching for a notepad on the counter. I wrote it down and read it back to Reagan to see if I had it right.

"Thanks, Al. I'll see you in the morning."

The number was busy the first time I called, but Johnson answered the second time. "This is Shiloh Tempest. How are you, Roy?"

"Good, Shiloh, for an old man with a bad back. I found a witness on the second canvas who said there was a guy hanging around the parking lot of Svenson's apartment the night of the murder. We have a composite now."

"Can you give me the description, then fax the composite to my department?"

"Sure. The witness said it was big guy, six-feet or better, husky with a full head of dark hair. My witness is real young, so she may or may not be right in her age estimate. She puts it somewhere between forty-five and fifty-five. That fit any suspect at your end?"

"Yes, it does, Roy. I appreciate the information. Do you need the fax number?"

"No, it's on the card you left. I'll get it on the way. If you think it's a close match to the composite, I'd appreciate a photo and name."

"You got it, Roy. Thanks. Wait, Roy! Before you hang up, did ATF dig up anything on the Colt pistol?"

"Yeah, we know exactly when and where it was made. We know who legally purchased it in Houston, Texas, but he's been dead thirty years. The weapon's stone cold, Shiloh."

"Thanks again, Roy."

I called Al Reagan back. "Al, go to records and pick up a fax that Sergeant Johnson is sending from Marietta. I don't want it passing through Rosenbaum's box."

"Consider it done, Loo."

With everything ready to go in the oven or ready to throw on the stove, I took my laptop into the sunroom and sat down in my recliner. I opened my laptop and went to a folder called *Book Fragments* and opened it. There were a dozen titles, ranging from thirty pages to nearly a hundred, all of them books I had started and abandoned over my four year dry spell — everything from science fiction to a book about my military service years.

One by one I opened them, looking for something that might catch fire, but I was no more interested than I had been when I abandoned them before. I sat back and relaxed. In fact, I became so relaxed that it was a little after six when I woke up.

Shaking off my nap, I went into the kitchen and turned on the oven. I washed the sweet potatoes, rubbed them with butter and wrapped them in aluminum foil. I went ahead and put them in the oven because they would take longer than the chops.

After that, I measured water for the instant stuffing, and set it on the back eye on high. I also emptied a can of green beans into small pot, added some butter, and set it on the eye, ready to heat ten minutes before it was time to serve dinner.

When the water was boiling, I took it off the stove and added the dry dressing. I found a sharp knife and slit the chops almost all the way through and stuffed them with the now-wet dressing. I located a small Pyrex baking dish, rubbed it with butter, and put the rest of the dressing into it.

I put the stuffed chops on top of the remaining dressing, covered it with aluminum foil and put it in the refrigerator. I would pop it in the oven at six-thirty. Jen was almost always home by seven.

I cleaned up, put the can from the green beans, the dressing box and the meat wrapper into the garbage pail. It was almost full, so I opened the door and stepped out on the back porch to empty it into the big can by the porch. The man crouched under my kitchen window, jumped up and sprinted around the corner of the house, into the small stand of trees by the house.

He was obviously in better condition for running than I was. The black hooded jersey he was wearing had obscured his face. I went back in the kitchen and picked up my Glock 26 off the table where I had put it when I brought the groceries in, got a flashlight from a drawer where I always kept one and went back out into the gathering twilight to look around.

I saw the headlights of Jennifer's car coming up the driveway and went back inside to pop the pork chops into the oven. The sweet potatoes were sizzling inside their aluminum foil jackets, so they were almost done. I was turning on the green beans as Jennifer came through the door from the garage.

"My, oh my," she said. "The chef has returned." She came over and kissed me on the lips. "Do I have time for a quick shower?"

"I could be persuaded to hold off a few minutes, assuming there was quid pro quo involved," and slapped her bottom lightly as she went down the hall giggling. As soon as she was in the shower, I scrolled the numbers in my cell phone until I found the one I needed. I punched *Send* and waited.

"Freelance Security," a man said.

"Ed, this is Shiloh Tempest. How are you?"

"I'm good," he said. "How can I help you?" Ed is a direct man.

"I need heat and motion sensors all around my house, lights, cams and sound-effects hooked to a wireless console inside."

"Your house, the one off Connor Road?"

"That's the one. I'm willing to pay extra for a rush job."

"No extra charge to you for a rush job, Shiloh. Any preference on the brand names for the equipment?" he asked.

"Ed, put what you would put around your own house. This may be a serious matter."

"Shiloh, since you never had a security system, I *assumed* it was serious. Do you need a security officer on hand for a few days?"

"No, I don't think so. If somebody gets inside, I'll deal with it. I just don't want anyone to surprise me."

"Seven o'clock in the morning soon enough?" he asked.

"That would be good, Ed. I'll leave a key with your technician and he can leave it on the dining room table when he's done."

"You can leave it with me, Shiloh. I'll be doing this one myself."

"I owe you one, Ed."

"No, I'll still owe *you* long after this job is done."

"The past is water under the bridge, Ed. See you in the morning."

Jennifer came down the hall wearing a pale yellow gown so sheer as to be almost nonexistent, with nothing under it, drying her long, black hair.

"Wow!" I said.

"You like, *Señor?*" She twirled around once and placed her hands on her hips.

"*Sí, señora, me gusta!*" I replied "Have a seat and I'll serve dinner."

"Who were you on the phone with, some hussy?"

"It was Nurse Solly. She just can't turn me loose."

"No, really. Was it work?"

"No, it was Ed Bergman. He's coming in the morning to install a comprehensive security system."

"This seems to be short notice. Why?"

"I thought I might have seen somebody trying to look in the window."

"Bull, Shiloh! You *caught* somebody looking through the window. Do you know who it was? Do you think it has something to do with the case you're working?"

"Anything's possible, Jen." I put plates and silverware on the table for both of us. "I'm just getting cautious in my old age. Ed said he'd rush it for me and I took him up on it."

I put two potholders on the table and set the dishes with the stuffed chops and dressing and the green beans on the table, then took an oven mitt and plopped a sweet potato on both plates.

"Hmmm… smells delicious," Jennifer said. "I don't doubt that Ed agreed to do a rush job for you. He's been trying to repay you for sixteen years and you won't let him."

"All I did was my job, Jen. Nobody should be praised for doing what's expected."

"If it hadn't been for your going the extra mile, Ed Bergman would be doing life in the pen for killing that biker that was stalking his wife."

"A man is entitled to defend his home and family."

"But *you* did the investigation and gave the testimony that convinced the jury it was justifiable homicide, not second degree murder. He feels like he owes you. He's running a successful security business instead of doing hard time. Let him repay the debt however he wants."

"Let's dig in," I said, "while everything's hot." And we did. It was a sort of coming home dinner, though neither of us mentioned it.

As I was rinsing the dishes after dinner, handing them to Jen so she could put them in the dishwasher, she looked out the window. "The same car has passed three times in the last twenty minutes, Shiloh. Now it's parked across the street."

"I'll check it out," I said.

"What not have the sheriff's department send a patrol unit?" she said.

"It's probably nothing." I stuck my baby Glock 26 in my hip pocket, went out the back door and walked in the darkness down to the street, coming out behind the car. As I approached, I saw the *Freelance Security* sticker on the door. The officer was smoking a cigarette, watching me in the side mirror.

"Good evening," I said. "Do you have an assignment here officer?"

"Are you Shiloh Tempest?" he asked.

"Yes, I am."

"Then you and Jennifer are my assignment. Apparently Ed thinks very highly of you. It's my day off and I'm on overtime. Anything I need to know?"

"Just that anybody who comes after me will be armed and dangerous."

"I figured that. Ed has security officers for routine and serious. I'm one of the serious ones. If it's okay with you, I'll be walking the perimeter from time to time. I don't want you shooting me."

"You set up for a stakeout?" I asked.

"I've got the officer's friends with me — a big thermos of coffee and an igloo cooler. You can say I'm set up, yes, sir."

"Well, have a good night," I said.

"You too," he answered.

Back at the house, Jennifer was waiting at the front door. "Did Ed Bergman send somebody?"

"Yes, he did. We'll be watched over tonight by one of his best."

"He's a good man, Ed Bergman."

"Yes he is," I agreed.

TWENTY

The next morning I left Ed Bergman and a two-man crew installing the security system. He had me write out a code and give a copy to Jennifer so that whoever got home first would be able to enter without setting off the alarm.

"Leave the bill on the kitchen table," I told him, but he had only grunted in a noncommittal fashion. I would probably end up slipping his wife the cash before it was over. Favors were never something I willingly accepted when I was a cop. In all my years in law enforcement, I never ordered a cup of coffee I didn't have the money to pay for.

When I arrived at the office, Freed was already there with a bag of assorted biscuits with egg, cheese, bacon, sausage and ham. I saw that Regan had already arrived since there was a full pot of coffee.

"Morning, Loo," Freed said.

"Morning, John. You get your tooth fixed?"

"Yeah, I did. Cost me five hundred bucks for a crown."

"You having the pearl you broke your tooth on set into a tie tack?" I put a sugar cube in my cup and poured the hot, black coffee over it.

"Yeah, I am. You already talked to Reagan this morning?"

"No, I'm an excellent judge of men. It was what I expected you to do."

"You pulling my leg, Loo?"

"Yeah, I am. Al predicted you'd do it."

"Me and ol' Al have been working together too long. We're like a married couple, except we've been partners longer than any of my marriages lasted."

"You ever think of looking for a woman who resembles Al?"

"That's a cruel thing to say, Loo. Can you imagine a woman who looked like him?"

"A woman who looks like *who*?" Reagan came through the door into our small office as I was unwrapping a bacon, egg and cheese biscuit.

"Shiloh thinks my marriages would last longer if I married someone more like you," Freed said.

"That's a truly hideous thought," Reagan said. "You have a nice day off, Loo?"

"Until I found an unexpected visitor outside my kitchen window."

Reagan stopped and turned his burred head in my direction, staring straight at me through his rimless glasses. "I take it you didn't have your piece at hand, since I heard nothing about a shooting. I hope you're giving sufficient weight to the timing of this, Loo. *I've* been nervous since Svenson got popped."

"I'm treating it very seriously, Al. As we speak, a first class security system is being installed at my home."

"That's good, because I've been a cop too long to believe in coincidences. I think we're so close to the truth now about Cynthia's death, we've scared somebody dangerous — somebody who knows how to make a silencer and get hold of a cold pistol."

"I'm proceeding from that assumption, Al."

"Good. I don't want to break in a new supervisor." He reached into the bag and came out with a sausage and biscuit.

Reagan poured himself a cup of coffee, sat down at his desk and handed me the composite drawing sent by Roy Johnson from Marietta. "Loo, this looks an awful lot like Joshua Quinn."

Indeed, it did resemble him. A strong chin, a full head of dark hair and piercing eyes. I thought back to the night before. It had been a big man under my window. But his face had been obscured by the dark hood.

"Of course, it looks like Chief Stiffy, too," Freed said with a chuckle.

"I hadn't noticed, but you're right, John. It does bear a resemblance to our resident obsessive-compulsive chief of defectives," Reagan said around a bite of sausage and egg.

"Loo, Al tells me you're convinced that Gettlefinger's not our killer," Freed said.

"We'll wait on the DNA, but I don't *think* he killed Cynthia Quinn. He's a pervert but he's had ample opportunity and never got physical before. That we know of."

"We got in two more names off the composite on Quinn's flyers and billboards, Loo. Are we gonna keep running them down now that we've probably got a better composite?"

"Yes, we will. We can't make assumptions about where we are — and that is the composite Svenson gave us. We'll keep working the case until the evidence solves it."

"Loo, how about I take these two leads? They're both north and I have to be out that way so the dentist can check on my crown to make sure it's seated right," Freed said.

"Go ahead, John. Just bring a note from the dentist in case Rosenbaum wants it."

"All right…" he looked at me sharply "…dang it, Loo! You just pulled my leg again, didn't you?"

"I couldn't resist it, John"

The phone rang and Reagan picked it up. "Hold on." Al put his hand over the mouthpiece. "Loo, Robert Svenson's mother is outside. She wants to talk to you."

"Go get her and bring her back, Al."

"I'll be up to get her," Reagan told the secretary.

"Loo, I'm outta here. I'll see you later," Freed said.

"Watch your back, John."

I sipped my coffee and finished my sausage, egg and cheese biscuit before Reagan returned with Robert Svenson's mother. When they came in, I got up and extended my hand to a woman who was perhaps fifty, but could have passed for forty if she tried. Her hair was a chestnut color and her eyes were the same blue as her son's.

"Mrs. Svenson, let me express my regret at the loss of your son. I was able to speak with him shortly before his death. He seemed to be a fine young man." She took my hand and shook it firmly. A handshake says a lot about character.

"Yes, we talked almost every evening. Robert told me he had spoken to you and he thought you believed him when he said he didn't kill Cynthia."

"I did believe him, Mrs. Svenson."

"And your visit probably got him killed, didn't it"

Reagan glanced at me to see what my reaction would be.

"It's entirely possible that you're right, Mrs. Svenson."

"Thank you for not lying to me, Lieutenant. I don't blame you for doing your job, and I hope you won't rest until you catch my son's killer — and presumably Cynthia's killer, too. Robert loved that girl, you know."

"I suspected as much, and I assure you, if it's humanly possible, we will catch the man who killed Robert." I handed her the composite from Marietta. "Does this man look familiar, Mrs. Svenson?"

"It looks like Joshua Quinn," she said, without hesitation. "Is Josh Quinn a suspect?"

"This composite came from Marietta, from a witness who said she saw him hanging around the apartment complex the night Robert was killed. We check all leads, no matter how unlikely."

"So Josh Quinn *is* a suspect?"

"I didn't say that, Mrs. Svenson. I just said that we check all leads, no matter how unlikely. How well do you know the Quinns?"

"Emma and I went to church together when our children were small. I was divorced and Josh was gone most of the time on Navy business. He was a Navy SEAL, you know."

"No, I didn't know that."

"Yes, he was a team leader before he moved to the intelligence end of the business. Then he was home even less. I think Emma liked it best when he was gone, though."

"Mrs. Svenson, exactly what did Robert say the last time he called you?" I asked.

"He said he had seen someone he didn't want to talk to and that he'd be gone from his apartment until he got in touch with you. I couldn't get him to elaborate. I wish I had tried harder."

There seemed no proper response, so as usual, I made none.

"Well, Lieutenant, I appreciate your kindness. Catch the bastard who did this, please." Tears were forming in her eyes as she turned to leave. "No need to walk me out, Detective Reagan. I know the way."

Then she was gone, leaving the faint odor of lavender in the air.

"Shiloh, a former Navy Seal probably wouldn't have much trouble getting his hands on a cold pistol and a silencer," Reagan said.

"No, I don't imagine he would.

"Are you ready to go interview Emma Quinn, Al?"

"No time like the present," he replied.

The Quinns live in a gated community by Fort Loudon Lake. The view is spectacular. I imagined that the house and property probably were valued in the millions, but I don't really know anything about real estate at this economic level. It was a place inhabited by CEOs and presidents of corporations. With two *New York Times* bestsellers, I had never generated the kind of money it took to live here and probably would not have been interested anyway.

The door was answered by a maid. Both Reagan and I held up our identification and displayed the gold stars on our belts. "We need to speak with Emma Quinn," I said.

"Jus' a minute," the maid said and vanished down the hall.

"What's a house like this cost, Shiloh?" Reagan asked.

"I have no idea, Al. I never had occasion to check this kind of real estate."

The maid came to the door again. "Missus Quinn said to bring you out on the patio. She's having breakfast."

Darkened inside, with closed drapes, the house smelled of a wood polish I remembered my mother using when I was a child. The rooms did not appear to be really lived in. There was more of a museum atmosphere.

On the patio, Emma Quinn sat at a white wrought-iron table with a large umbrella over it. She was wearing a white silk head scarf, sunglasses and a matching gown. There was an open bottle of champagne chilling in an ice bucket on the table.

"Gentlemen," she said, "sit down. May I offer you a drink? Mornings are the time I drink Mimosas and Bloody Marys. I'm sure you've both had the more manly drink, a Bloody Mary. A Mimosa is — champagne and orange juice."

"We'll have to pass on the drinks," I said. "We just need to ask you a few questions?"

"I wondered when you would get around to talking to me, because it's obvious to everyone that you think Josh killed Cynthia. Josh, most especially, understands "

"Actually, we're just being thorough, Mrs. Quinn," Reagan said.

"Oh, please call me Emma. Lieutenant Tempest, let me compliment you on almost destroying Josh's face. It's been a long time since anyone hurt and humiliated him the way you did." She took a deep swallow of the champagne and orange juice mix.

"Don't look at me like that, Detectives. Of course, I'm a little drunk. Josh locked me in my bedroom before we came to the sheriff's department to make sure I'd be sober."

"Emma, what kind of cars do you personally drive?" Reagan asked.

"I have a Lexus convertible and a classic Mercedes roadster. Josh drives that massive Escalade because it's more macho, I suppose. He also has a couple of restored Triumph sports cars to impress the ladies and his colleagues."

"What kind of relationship did your husband have with Cynthia?"

"Until she was fourteen, they were inseparable. After that, she avoided him like the plague," she said, draining the champagne glass and reaching for the pitcher to pour another.

"Did you not find that odd, Emma?" I asked.

"Of course I found it odd! I'm not stupid. I asked Cynthia about it, and gave her every opportunity to tell me if something was wrong. But she and I had never been as close as I would have liked because Josh showered so much attention on her and let her have her way without regard for my opinion."

"Did your husband have a key to Cynthia's apartment?" I asked.

"No."

"I understand that you did?"

"Yes, Lieutenant. I had a key. When Cynthia had the flu, I took care of her for a week and that's when she gave me the key."

"Is it possible your husband had a key made?" Reagan inquired.

"Gentlemen, anything's possible. Joshua Quinn is manipulative, controlling and a total asshole. Whether he's a murderer and sexual predator, I don't know."

"The weekend of Cynthia's death, your husband was in Chattanooga…"

"Yes, he was. No doubt drinking too much, fighting and sleeping with whores. That's his normal behavior," Emma said.

"The night Cynthia was murdered, a red-light camera caught your husband's Escalade running a light on Kingston Pike, not far from where she died," I told her.

"Then you also know I paid the ticket with one of my checks."

"Yes, we knew that. But we didn't think he would have had any trouble getting you to cover for him." I said.

"Josh never knew about the ticket," she said, taking another long swallow from the champagne glass. "I was driving the Escalade that night. Josh took one of his restored Triumph sports car to impress his old Navy buddies."

"Emma, you don't have to cover for him any longer," I said.

"I'm *not* covering for him. Right before I ran the red-light, I had been parked in a Wal-Mart parking lot, having my brains screwed out by a young waiter from a Ruby Tuesday restaurant. Knowing I'm betraying Joshua in his own precious and manly SUV on steroids gives me an extra thrill." Emma poured herself another drink.

We sat quietly for perhaps thirty seconds. Then Reagan removed a small notepad from his shirt pocket and laid the pad and a pen in front of Emma Quinn. "We'll need his name and a place where we can reach him, Emma." She scribbled on the pad and handed it back.

"Emma, just out of curiosity, why have you stayed with your husband so long in what is obviously a war rather than a marriage. You've been married a long time and you could come out of a divorce with a substantial settlement," I said.

"Perhaps it's because I'd have to drink domestic champagne in my Mimosas instead of *Louis Roederer*, Lieutenant. Or maybe I enjoy the twisted relationship."

"We thank you for time, Emma. You've been very helpful," I said. "You secret will remain secret with us."

"I never doubted that for a moment, Lieutenant," she replied. "Both of you are gentlemen and you remind me that chivalry is not dead."

TWENTY-ONE

Three basic plots, infinite variations. Writing a murder mystery and investigating a murder are very similar in some ways. To put together a good case, cops have to come up with motive and opportunity, at the least, along with all the hard evidence they can find. All the suspects that Reagan, Freed and I had investigated fell under the same inflexible rules.

David West had motive, and it was anger over being spurned as a suitor, but we had eliminated opportunity when we found out he was doing a burglary in Hickory, North Carolina, at the time of the murder. Now he was in North Carolina awaiting trial on burglary, but he wasn't our killer.

David Gettlefinger had opportunity, but we had pretty much eliminated motive. He is a voyeur, but Cynthia Quinn hadn't know she was being watched and he had no reason to eliminate her. Besides, we had found the receipt for the camera in one of his shoeboxes. To me, he had seemed the most likely suspect.

Josh Quinn had motive, also. It was possessiveness and lust, but Emma Quinn had removed opportunity when she gave us the name of the young man she was making love to in the back of her husband's prized vehicle.

Her young lover had verified her story. It didn't entirely eliminate Quinn since he still could have driven to Knoxville without being noticed, but for all practical purposes, he was out. Of course, we were still waiting on his DNA results.

As far as cold, hard evidence went, we were back to square one. None of our basic plots had congealed. *Someone* had motive and opportunity, but they had not left a shred of evidence that would stand up in court, assuming we had gotten a case to court. District Attorneys don't like losing cases and they have the final say on prosecution.

I was sipping my morning coffee, going through the files, looking for something we had missed, when the office phone rang. I answered, "Hello, Tempest speaking."

"Shiloh, this is Roy Johnson from Marietta."

"How's your case coming together, Roy?"

"I used the two pictures you sent by overnight mail earlier this week in a picture line-up. The witness went straight to the one you labeled 'B' as the guy hanging around Svenson's apartment complex. We showed the picture around the neighborhood and a waitress at the coffee shop down from Robert Svenson's job site said this guy was in the shop the same day Svenson was killed."

"Are you sure it was picture 'B' and not 'A?'" I asked.

"Of course, I'm sure. Do you have this guy in custody? I need to interview him."

"No, he's not in custody. Can you give me until noon tomorrow and then call back, Roy? I have some stuff I need to put together today."

"Sure, I'll get back with you tomorrow. Thanks for the pictures, Shiloh."

"Not a problem, Roy. I'm glad I could help."

"Damn," I said to myself. "This would make *bad* fiction." I opened my desk drawer and took out the file folder I had been carrying home with me every night, the one even Freed and Reagan hadn't seen, then called upstairs. "Madeline, is the Sheriff in his office?"

"Yes. Do you need to see him?"

"I do, and I think you need to clear his appointments for a couple of hours."

I left a note for Reagan and Freed not to leave the office until I returned, then walked down the long hallway to the elevators, carrying the folder with me. At the Sheriff's door, Madeline waved me in.

Sam was shuffling through a stack of papers, dressed in a knit shirt with the department logo on it and khaki pants. I went to the chair in front of his desk and tossed my pack of Camel filters to him.

He looked at the pack, then reached into his desk drawer and set out the ashtray and butane lighter with a sigh. "Shiloh, I'm supposed to play in a celebrity golf tournament this morning for charity. The Governor and a U.S. Senator are going to be there. Don't tell me you're going to ruin it for me. I need the governor's support."

"There's no reason you can't play golf, Sam. We'll be getting some paper signed by a judge and putting things together until well into the afternoon hours. I would like to have you on hand at five, though, when we do the interview. But I can't promise you that you'll play your best game today after you see what I have."

Sam lit one of my cigarettes and said, "Show me."

I opened the folder and laid out each document, one by one, explaining how I had obtained them and why. The Sheriff's face grew darker with every new detail, until I had presented my full case.

"You're too good a cop not to know that you don't have a shred of physical evidence here, Shiloh. Are you sure you don't want to hold off until you've got something you can actually take to court?"

"Most cases start with a theory, Sam. Hopefully, we will have more physical evidence as the thing unfolds. But if I don't act now, the Marietta investigation is going to tip him off and give him time to get rid of evidence."

"How can I help?" Sam said, putting out the cigarette, then lighting another.

"Tell him you want him to sit in on an interrogation at five."

"This is going to look bad, Shiloh." Sam took a deep drag on the cigarette.

"It's going to look worse if it comes out some other way, Sam."

"All right. Get what you need together. I'm not going to wish you luck because I hope you're wrong. I'll be trying to act cheerful this morning in front of the Governor, knowing what's going down today."

"Sorry, Sam."

"Don't be sorry. I brought you in to do a job because I knew you would."

Freed, Reagan and I walked the short distance to Rosenbaum's office at a quarter to five that afternoon. We stopped outside his office and I said, "Chief, the Sheriff told us you'll be sitting in on this interview."

He looked up and there was a slight sneer on his face: "How does it feel to have the Sheriff go over *your* head, Lieutenant?"

"He *is* the Sheriff," I said. "I can do what he says or I can quit. If he wants to make you privy to a case, it's his choice."

"Now you've figured it out, Lieutenant." Rosenbaum looked at the three of us, saw that we had empty holsters, then locked his Glock pistol in a desk drawer.

We walked to the center of the building together and got on the elevator. As we started down the hall to the interrogation room, Rosenbaum stopped in front of the small restroom that had originally been installed for records' personnel. "I need to take a leak."

The three of us waited outside until we heard a flush and the sink running. As we approached the interrogation room, Rosenbaum commented on the two armed officers outside. To me they looked like Tweedledum and Tweedledee, barrel chested and heads shaved, but their name tags said Kline and Smith. "Your suspect must be pretty dangerous."

"We think so, Chief."

"I didn't know the Sheriff was sitting in on this, too," Rosenbaum said, as he looked through the one-way mirror.

Freed opened the door to the interrogation room and said, "Age before beauty, gentlemen."

We all entered and Reagan locked the door behind us. "Chief, put your hands on the wall and spread'em"

"What is this?" Rosenbaum said, looking at our faces.

"Do as he says, Tim," Sam Renfro said. He was still wearing his golf togs.

Rosenbaum did as he was told and Reagan shook him down, thoroughly, even to the shake of the genitals with the back of his hand. "He's clean," the big detective said.

"I would expect this from Shiloh Tempest, Sheriff, but I expected better from you," Rosenbaum said.

"Sit down, Tim. Let's get this over with as soon as possible," the Sheriff said, and Rosenbaum sat. The Sheriff nodded for me to begin.

"The first question I have for you is: what were your whereabouts were on the night Cynthia Quinn was stabbed to death?"

"Cynthia Quinn? I didn't even know who she was until she was murdered."

"Yes, you did. You met her when she came in to pick up her purse that was stolen in a burglary of her car in February of that year. You signed off on the release form and that's probably when you got her keys.

"She's just the type of woman you prey on. Petite, pretty, with a waif-like quality about her — a lot like the one who almost cost you your job when you were still a patrol sergeant and a lot like all three of your wives.

"You had words with Cynthia at the drug store right before she was killed. She brushed you off. There was a video of the argument you had. It was poor quality, and we were focused on Joshua Quinn. It wasn't until I saw you and Quinn side by side in the Sheriff's office that I was struck by the resemblance.

"Now, answer the question. Where were you the night Cynthia Quinn was stabbed to death in her apartment?"

"I was at home, packing for a trip to Daytona. You're really grasping at straws, Tempest."

"Actually, you didn't book the flight to Daytona until after eleven the night Cynthia was murdered," I said, "and you didn't call the office to have your schedule changed until the next morning. You hadn't planned a vacation until a month later. You were booked for a criminal profiling seminar in Lexington, Virginia. Your trip to Daytona was spur of the moment."

"So? It's not against the law to be spontaneous."

"No, it isn't, but it does run contrary to your obsessive-compulsive nature, Rosenbaum. The only reason you ever abandon a plan is if it's forced on you.

"When you went into Cynthia Quinn's apartment that night, you were convinced, despite everything she had said to the contrary, that she would welcome you with open arms. It's your fantasy that women find you irresistible. But not only did she push you away, she was sleeping with a butcher knife because of her nightmares and maybe her memories.

"All you intended to do was show her how a *real* man makes love, but you had to kill her when she started fighting, and you cut your hand on that wet, slippery butcher knife while you were stabbing her or Robert Svenson. After that, you were *forced* to improvise, and you did a pretty good job."

"Now Tempest is a psychologist *and* a psychic, Sheriff? Can't you see through what he's trying to do here? He's power hungry, Sam!" Rosenbaum said.

"In Daytona, you checked into the Bermuda House Hotel. The desk clerk remembered you because you were so agitated — and because you had your right hand wrapped in gauze."

"Yes, I *was* there, but it was the *next* day when my hand was bandaged, after the shark bite, which I had stitched up at an emergency room — an incident that made the newspaper."

"I talked to the emergency room doctor who stitched you up, Rosenbaum. *He* didn't say you had a shark bite, you did. As a matter of fact, he had his doubts. *You* called the press and told them that a shark had grabbed your hand. On a slow news day an out-of-town chief of detectives bitten by a shark looked good.

"I also talked to the officer you reported the bite to. His report says that nobody witnessed the alleged shark attack. You just walked up to him on the beach carrying your fishing gear and *told* him it had happened.

"The paramedic who first treated you on the way to the hospital said in her report that you had a deep gash across your palm but only minor scratches across the back of your hand. In fact, her report said the gash appeared too clean to have been consistent with a shark bite."

"Is this what you called me in for, Tempest? You've put together all these suppositions and theories, but you don't have a *shred* of evidence. You must really be desperate," Rosenbaum said. "You don't have a case here. You don't even have a sustainable theory. I have half a mind to walk out of here."

"No, you *won't* walk out of here until we're finished, Tim," Sam Renfro said. "If you do, your career is over. Even your political pull won't save you if you leave."

"The maintenance man at the Bermuda House Hotel remembered you very well, Rosenbaum, and he should. You gave him over five hundred dollars worth of what he described as 'brand new' fishing gear, including a rod and reel, tackle box and accessories before you left."

"So I'm a generous man," Rosenbaum said. "I knew I wasn't going to do any more surf fishing after the shark grabbed me. I had no use for the stuff after that."

"The next question we have for you, Chief Rosenbaum, is: where were you on the night Robert Svenson was executed?" I said.

"I didn't even know he was dead." He turned to the Sheriff. "They've kept me completely out of the loop on this, Sam."

"You signed off when I took my department car to Marietta the first time, Rosenbaum. You knew where I'd been and you knew where Robert Svenson was because you had access to the files until I took over.

"You *didn't* sign off on my second Marietta trip because you weren't at work. Reagan looked for you but you weren't on the job. You did make a big ruckus over my trip the *next* day."

"I took a day off because I wasn't feeling well, but I was at home the entire time,' Rosenbaum said.

"Well, according to the station where you fill up your department car, you topped it off that afternoon, then put twenty gallons in the tank again the next morning." I said. "You had plenty of time to go to Marietta and back."

"Okay, so I ran a few errands when I was off sick. It's a technical violation, but everyone does it. I'll pay for the tank of gas."

"That might fly, Rosenbaum, but two eyewitnesses put you in Marietta the night of Robert Svenson's murder. One at the apartment complex where he lived and the other at the coffee shop down from his place of employment.

"He saw you at the coffee shop, didn't he, Rosenbaum? The night you killed Cynthia Quinn and *tried* to kill him, and told him he'd better keep his mouth shut if he wanted to live. Then you insisted on doing the polygraph to make sure he *remembered* that his life depended on forgetting your name."

Rosenbaum snorted in feigned disgust. "Weave your fantasy, Tempest."

"Robert had packed to leave his apartment that night, but you caught him when he opened the door and silenced him for good."

"Tempest, this sounds a lot like one of your cheap thrillers, but nobody saw me in Marietta, Georgia, because I haven't been there."

"Sure you have, and your picture has been there. The detective working the case in Marietta showed it around. He's coming up to interview you. And by the way, *we* need a sample of *your* DNA, Rosenbaum."

"Get a warrant," he said.

"We already have,' I told him.

"I've had all this I'm going to take." Rosenbaum stood up. "Charge me or I'm gone."

"All right, Timothy James Rosenbaum, you're under arrest for the murder of Cynthia Quinn, and on hold for suspicion in the murder of Robert Svenson until the Marietta authorities get here. Cuff him, Detectives."

"You have no probable cause," he snarled.

"Actually, we have sufficient evidence to lead a reasonable person to believe a crime has been committed. You've read the text book the same as I have. That's the definition, isn't it?

"Forensics is executing a search warrant on your house as we speak, Timmy," I said. "As obsessive and compulsive as you are, we'll have hard evidence by tomorrow because you stash away *everything*, usually in alphabetical order."

"And you're suspended without pay, pending investigation," the Sheriff said.

"You're all going to regret this — especially you, Tempest!"

"Just don't be looking in my kitchen window again, Rosenbaum."

Reagan opened the door and spoke to the two uniformed officers. "Take Chief Rosenbaum down and have the jail start processing him. Tell them he's on hold, per Lieutenant Tempest. Make sure he's segregated. We don't want anything to happen to our chief of detectives. Also take him by medical to get a DNA swab. Here's the court order for the nurse."

When they had taken Rosenbaum away, we all sat at the table, not speaking for a couple of minutes. Finally Sam Renfro broke the silence. "Shiloh, I hope this doesn't collapse like a house of cards."

"He did it, Sam," I replied.

"I think you're right, but if the search warrant for his house and the one for his DNA don't hold up, the case is dead in the water. If Judge Stanton hadn't known you personally, he would never have signed either warrant. You know that, don't you?"

"Yes, I know it, Sam. But right now, Rosenbaum is not in a position to hurt anyone else — and I have great faith in sociopaths to be their own worst enemies. They don't believe in justice. I do."

"I hope you're right, Shiloh. We have a lot riding on it," Sam said.

"Well," I said, "we all have better things to do than sit around here."

Everyone nodded and we all stood. It was at that moment that the door opened and Kline, one of the large, husky patrol officers who had just escorted Rosenbaum away, burst in. He was breathing heavily.

"He got away!" the officer said.

"How?" the Sheriff asked.

"He told us he had to take a leak at the little restroom by records," the obviously agitated patrol officer said. "It's small and there's no way out, so we took one of the cuffs loose. He came out with a little automatic pistol and made us walk him out the side door to the lobby. He took our weapons and he's gone."

"He got suspicious," Reagan said, "and planted a pistol in the restroom on the way here. We should have expected it from that cunning sonofabitch!"

"You were right, Shiloh. He *didn't* trust the system, and now he's nailed himself to the cross. One of you call dispatch and BOLO his name and description." Sam Renfro said.

By the time the BOLO was out, we had talked to building security. Rosenbaum had walked out slowly through the lobby, arousing no attention, and had gone out the main door on L-1, right by the security office. He had tossed the weapons taken from his escorts into a garbage can by the door. The security officer on duty thought Rosenbaum *might* have gotten into a late-model white Toyota Corolla parked by the curb, driven by someone waiting to pick up a passenger, but he wasn't sure.

Less than an hour later, when we were in the process of warning our own family members and his former wives that Rosenbaum was out on the streets and had nothing to lose, someone shot his estranged wife and her parents through the head, execution style. The shooter didn't clean up the shell casings and they were the kind used by all officers of the sheriff's department.

A white Toyota Corolla was found parked at a used-car lot near the scene of the murder, with the registered owner dead in the trunk. The manager of the car lot said he was missing a beat-up old Plymouth. And Rosenbaum had vanished.

TWENTY-TWO

The individual in conflict with other individuals; the individual in conflict with himself; the individual in conflict with the forces of nature, which had made him less than he aspired to be. Tim Rosenbaum was all these things.

There's a difference between psychopaths and sociopaths. The social scientists will tell you that one cannot help what he is doing and the other doesn't care what he is doing. From the police point of view, it doesn't matter which label is used. Either way, cops are tracking an individual who does not operate on the same frequency as those of us who have a conscience, or they cannot feel the pain of others.

Reagan had sent his wife to a safe place and I had done the same for Jennifer. Sam Renfro was being tailed by officers at all times and I had ordered Freed to bunk at Reagan's house until we caught Rosenbaum. We alerted everyone, including the former chief of detective's ex-wives, who might be targets, and could only hope they had listened. Extra guards were on duty all over the City-County Building.

Tim Rosenbaum's house and tool shed had yielded more than we ever expected. There were three more silencers he had made in a small machine shop in his basement. His stash of pornography, dedicated to the rape and humiliation of small, waif-like women resembling his three wives, Cynthia Quinn and the young woman who had accused him of attacking her when he was still a patrol sergeant, was massive.

We speculated that there were probably dozens of abused women of whom we had no knowledge, scattered around the country, in places where he had gone for seminars and police schools. Most victims don't file reports.

We found long, rambling, badly-written manuscripts of novels he had authored, dealing primarily with the abuse and humiliation of women, with himself as the central character, an international operative in a secret world that only he understood. There were disguises — beards, wigs, mustaches and professional make-up — and Polaroids of Rosenbaum wearing them.

He had become quite adept at disguising himself. Reagan wondered aloud why he had not disguised himself in Marietta, then answered his own question; he didn't expect to see anyone he knew.

He had a small library on the art of vanishing without a trace, and documents from around the country which he had apparently used to apply for Social Security numbers, driver's licenses and other forms of identification.

Tucked in with the other things were instruction manuals for foiling electronic alarm systems, explosives manuals, locksmithing and even a formula for a nicotine-based poison for a blowgun he was holding in one of the Polaroids. We also found two automatic rifles he had converted from semiautomatics and several handguns.

Every day for 28 years arousing raising no suspicion — other than for his sometimes clownish obsessive-compulsive behavior — that at night he lived in a world in which he was a shadow man, a dark anti-hero, watching the rest of humanity, all of whom were there for his amusement and use. A man in conflict with the rest of us and with what he thought himself to be.

The most frightening thing for me personally were the pictures he had shot through my windows, beginning the day I had taken over the Quinn case. There were pictures of Jennifer and me in our sunroom and pictures of both of us standing at the kitchen window where I had found him crouching one evening.

I was looking through some of the documents found at Rosenbaum's house when Sheriff Renfro came into our crowded little office.

"You busy, Shiloh?" he asked, pausing at the door.

"I'm busy with an exercise in futility," I said, "But I can go back to that at any time."

"Rosenbaum is making us look like idiots. We have to run him to ground."

"We're doing everything we can, Sam." I said. "The three of us putting in twelve hour days, every day."

"I know that. I want you to move into Rosenbaum's office to run the investigation. I'll assign half the detectives of this department to work with you and Reagan and Freed. I should have done it a week ago when he escaped, but I thought we'd have run him to ground before this."

"All right, Sam. You're the Sheriff."

"I also want to announce today that you're my new chief of detectives. I'll make a big media event of it. That should bring a major reaction. Maybe he'll get careless."

"I'd say you're right, Sam. The idea of having me sit in his chair will be like insult piled upon injury as far as he's concerned."

"I know it will put a target on your back, Shiloh. You don't have to do it. All you signed on for was to catch Cynthia Quinn's killer. You've done that and you're not obligated any further."

"I *already* have a target on my back, Sam. And I'm worried about innocent people who might become collateral damage, especially Jennifer. He was stalking us *before* we exposed him. If you think this will help flush him out, make me chief of detectives — but understand it's only until we bring in Rosenbaum."

"Understood. I'll have a crew start taking down Rosenbaum's personal stuff. You tell them what you want moved from here. And I'll get on the phone to the news media."

The media event went off without a hitch. My promotion to chief of detectives was carried in the newspaper and on three television stations. It was only twenty-four hours later when my office phone rang.

"Hello. Tempest speaking."

"So you finally got what you wanted, Tempest. We'll see if it was worth the price in blood that's going to be on your conscience."

I hit the button to initiate a trace of the call. Todd Culvahouse had set up a system the day after Rosenbaum escaped and went underground.

"Why don't you come in?" I said. "You're never going to have any peace until you do. You have no place to go where we can't find you."

"I seem to be doing all right now, don't I? I had *years* to prepare. The stuff you stole from my house was just a fraction of what I have. By the way, don't bother trying to trace this call. It's a throwaway cell phone and I'm on the move."

"This is all pointless, Tim. Come in and let us help you."

"So now it's *Tim*. Is that right, *Chief?* Now you can be kind because you have what you always wanted? You have *my* job."

"I never wanted this job, Tim. It was all in your mind."

"Well, I have a present for you and it's *not* all in my mind. Write down this address." He reeled off an address that I recognized as the University of Tennessee area. I motioned for my secretary and handed her the address, under which I had written, *"Rosenbaum, call dispatch and give them this address. Possible armed suspect."*

"What's your plan here, Tim? What do you hope to accomplish?"

"Payback, Tempest. Payback for every bastard who ever screwed me. It's a long list, but I have plenty of time! By the way, my *next* present to you will be an old cop.

"Oh, almost forgot, I hope you thieves got all you wanted from my house because it's gone. I just burned it." I heard a whooshing sound, followed by a clunk and the phone went dead. He had apparently tossed it out the window.

I switched my radio to the Knoxville Police Department main channel, just in time to hear KPD arrive at the address Rosenbaum had given me. Moments later, Freed and Reagan came through my office door.

"Todd said you just activated the phone trace. He called our office by mistake. Have you heard from Rosenbaum?" Reagan asked.

"Listen," I said, nodding at the portable radio on my desk,

The KPD officer on the scene called for an ambulance and a homicide investigator, then put out a BOLO for a homeless man on a bicycle, describing him as tall, shaggy and armed and dangerous.

Todd Culvahouse came into my office and said, "Lieutenant, he didn't stay on long enough for me to get a fix."

"I think he tossed it out the window of his car, anyway," I replied. "Rosenbaum indicated that he has killed someone in the U.T. area. He gave me an address there and KPD's on the scene calling for an ambulance and homicide officer.

As I was speaking, another KPD officer found the bicycle ridden by the so-called homeless man. It had been abandoned behind a restaurant a few blocks away. I picked up my phone and called dispatch. "This is Chief Tempest.

Patch me through to the KPD officer on the scene at the Laurel Avenue location. I'll wait."

"If Rosenbaum did this, his body count's up to six now," Freed said.

"Excuse me," I said, putting the phone on speaker as dispatch patched the officer through. "Officer Goin, this is Chief Tempest at the sheriff's department. Do you have a name and cause of death on your victim yet?"

"Chief, it's a retired Professor Daniel Lewis. Looks like two rounds to the head and four to the body. Appears to be .22 caliber wounds. His wife says she was in the back bedroom and heard the doorbell but no shots. This old man apparently just opened the door and was shot without warning. The victim is eighty-three years old, Chief."

"Thanks, Officer. Have homicide call me when they get there. I think I know who the shooter is." I tuned off the phone and slammed my fist down on the desk. "Damn him! The sick twisted bastard. Damn him! He says his next *gift* to me will be an old cop. And we must not have gotten all his silencers. He apparently just used another one."

"I'll have personnel start notifying retired officers to be on the watch for him," Freed said. I nodded assent. "John, check with Rural Metro, too. Rosenbaum says he just torched his house."

"We're doing everything we can, Shiloh. We can't start blaming ourselves. Nobody had any idea what kind of monster Rosenbaum really was," Reagan said.

"I may have something useful I pulled off his computer's hard drive this morning," Culvahouse said.

"What is it?" I asked.

"Plans for some type of square concrete building. I don't have a location yet to go with the plans. Rosenbaum ran a professional-grade program to delete files and obviously used it regularly. I'm only pulling up things in small pieces. It's slow going."

"Keep at it, Todd. I appreciate everything you're doing," I told him.

"Chief, would you like to go for a few beers with me and Freed after work. I think you could use a little R and R," Reagan said.

"I appreciate the offer, Al. But I'm taking Jennifer to dinner tonight. I hope you're staying in regular touch with your wife. It's important to stay in touch."

"I am, Shiloh. Fortunately, my wife doesn't work outside the house. She's enjoying her visit with family up in West Virginia."

"You and Freed getting on each other's nerves yet?"

"Nope, and the house is cleaner than it's been in years. That boy won't go to bed if there's a dirty dish in the sink."

Jennifer came out the front from the lobby of the twenty-story office building on Gay Street where her firm occupies two floors. The security officer in the lobby with her waved at me. I watched with admiration as she walked to the car, clad in an aquamarine pants suit and opened the car door. She appeared to glide rather than walk. Women who looked like her had sent conquistadors across oceans in search of fame and fortune.

"Hello, Chief Tempest, it's good to see you." She leaned over and gave me a quick but warm and wet kiss.

"Don't get fond of the title; it's only until we catch Rosenbaum." I pulled away from the curb, crossed over to the turning lane and made a left. At Henley Street I turned left again, watching my rearview mirror.

"And how is that going?" she asked.

"The technician found a file on Rosenbaum's laptop computer that we hope will lead us to where he's hiding out," I said.

"Was he involved in the murder on Laurel Avenue today?"

"Why would you think that?"

"I work in a *law* office, Shiloh. People talk. Did Rosenbaum do it or not?"

"He probably did."

"And what crime did that elderly man commit against Rosenbaum?"

"He accused Rosenbaum of plagiarism and blocked his master's thesis more than twenty-five years ago," I answered reluctantly.

"What's his body count now?" Jennifer asked.

"We think it's six. He was disguised as a homeless man on a bicycle today. Nobody looks at a homeless person. By the time a connection was made, Rosenbaum had vanished again."

"Besides you, who else do you think is on his list?"

"We're assuming anybody he's ever been in contact with is at risk. His other two ex-wives, retired police officers, *anybody* could be targeted. We don't know how his mind works because his breed isn't fully human.

"How does dinner at Bayou Bay sound tonight?" I asked before she could question me further.

"It's as good as any place else," she said.

"How are you getting along with your roommate? A partner, right?"

"Yes, and she's very kind. The rest of the firm is making sure I have a ride everywhere I need to go and an armed escort when I'm in court."

"It's not going to last forever, Jen. We'll be back home very soon."

"Not soon enough to suit me," she said.

Joshua Quinn approached my office and rapped lightly on the partially-open door. He had stopped at the front desk and asked to see me. "Come in," I said. He came in uncertainly and stood in front of my desk until I motioned for him to pull up a chair.

"Lieutenant... I mean *Chief* Tempest, I wanted to come by and thank you for finding Cynthia's killer. Sheriff Renfro called me at home before the story about Rosenbaum hit the news. I really appreciate it."

"Mister Quinn, I don't expect praise for doing what's expected of me, but I appreciate it nonetheless." I picked up an envelope that had been on my desk for a couple of days, took the letter out and handed it to him.

He examined it for a moment, then said, "I'm not on up police technology, but this looks like the results of a DNA test."

"It is," I answered. "It's a sample of your DNA compared to the DNA from the third party in Cynthia's apartment the night she was murdered."

"How did you get it?" he asked.

"You left it all over my shirt in the Sheriff's office."

"Oh, *I see.* I thought you were just being cruel. You had a reason, though."

153

"Just out of curiosity, why didn't you voluntarily give up a sample? It would have made things a lot simpler for everyone."

"There was a possibility that the sample of my DNA might have revealed that I was Cynthia's real father."

"You were sleeping with your *brother's* wife?"

"I know. I'm a loathsome man. But my wife, Emma, has been faithful to me for thirty years. I'm the only man she's ever been with. I didn't want her to find out I was unfaithful — especially not with my brother's wife. Can you understand that?"

I stared at him for a moment, thinking of what his wife had told me and Reagan during her interview. *As you sow, therefore shall you reap*, I thought. "Well," I finally said, "the Bible says a good woman is a pearl without price."

Todd Culvahouse came to my office door before Quinn could reply. "Chief, I may have something for you."

"Mister Quinn, thanks for stopping by. I need to get back to work."

When Quinn was gone, Todd handed me a piece of paper with an address on it. "I think this is the address associated with the building plans Rosenbaum had on his laptop.

"It's in Union County. I called the Register of Deeds over there and the property is registered to a Ross Hollifield. There's no paper trail for anyone by that name

"Thanks, Todd. If this pans out I'll dance at your wedding and ask the Sheriff to give you a raise."

TWENTY-THREE

"All right, gentlemen and ladies, we're going to make this quick but thorough," I said to the fifteen detectives assembled in the rollcall room. We were all dressed in work clothes that might be worn by farmers or factory workers. "Does everyone have a picture of Tim Rosenbaum as himself and in the two other disguises?"

"Chief, how did he do this one where he has no upper teeth in front? It looks real." A detective named Raz Wilson asked.

"He had his front teeth knocked out by a drunk named John Lindsey with a two-by-four in 1985. He's been wearing a partial plate since then."

"Chief, you worked with Rosenbaum on the streets. Is he a pogue?" Wilson asked

"No, he isn't. He never let anyone go through a door before him. He's sick and twisted beyond belief, but he's not a coward and he's dangerous. Now, pay attention.

"This is an aerial photograph shot from our own helicopter of the Beard Valley area. Right here is where we think Rosenbaum is. Here's a house trailer, and about fifty yards behind it is a square concrete structure. It looks like a bunker and it may be. No plans were ever filed on its construction.

"Rosenbaum told me that what we had seized from his house is nothing compared to what he still has. We found two fully automatic rifles, several handguns, three silencers and a formula for nicotine poison to be used for darts in a blow gun. Let your imagination be your guide.

"The target has not left his compound in two days. We rented an old house on the ridge across from his place and have a surveillance team watching from there, so we'll know if he moves. If he does move, we'll try to take him in an area with as few people as possible, but he doesn't seem to leave the concrete building very often, except to pick up things from the trailer.

"What we want to do this morning, as unobtrusively as possible, is show these pictures around at all the businesses up and down Highway 33 from the county line to Maynardville to see if anyone recognizes Rosenbaum. What we want is intelligence. We already have a search warrant to execute on his property, but if there's anything we can learn today, we need to learn it. This man has logged a body count of six that we know of."

"At noon, we rendezvous at this staging point with the Union County officers, behind this quarry. They don't know where we're going so they can't let anything slip. But they know the area better than we do. Treat them with respect — no big city cop posturing.

A tall thin detective named Woodard whom I knew only slightly raised his hand. "Chief, why don't we just surround this guy, then swoop in on him? We got enough people."

"Woodard, haven't you been listening? This man is a sociopath or psychopath, a highly-trained police officer and a stone killer. He's attended every police school in America and has schooled himself in electronics and explosives. He kills people the way you'd swat bugs. We're trying to minimize our chances of walking into a trap."

"A one man trap, Chief? Come on." Woodard snickered.

"You're relieved, Woodard. Report to Lieutenant Robison for general assignment duty. I don't need you today."

"I'm a member of the SWAT team," Woodard said indignantly. "You need me."

"This isn't a SWAT team operation, Woodard. You're excused."

The other detectives watched the angry detective stalk out of the room. "Is everyone else on the same page here?" I asked. "This is not a day for heroics. We really have no idea what we're going to find when we get there."

I went back to the white board. "Here is an old logging road. Team B, under Detective Reagan's command, will be led into position by Union County officers. Nobody is to get closer than two hundred yards until I give the go-ahead. If he bolts, that team will be in position to take him

"I'll be in command of Team A. When I give the go-ahead, we will go up the gravel drive in vehicles, off Beard Valley Road, fan out and take cover. I want him alive if at all possible.

"Do all of you understand what we're doing and where the rendezvous point is?"

They nodded but nobody else spoke. "Good. We've got five hours to gather intel. I'll see everyone at the rendezvous point at noon. Low profile is the uniform of the day."

The entire squad was at the rendezvous point by noon, including the Union County officers. Most were drinking soft drinks and a few were eating sandwiches they had brought from home or munching on cheeseburgers or takeout chicken.

"Everybody gather round me over here under the tree so we'll have a little shade. It will be hot for the next few hours."

They sauntered over in the manner of American police officers everywhere, taking their time and hiding their anxieties. Finally we were all gathered under the tree.

"How many of you had people identify our suspect?"

Almost every officer raised his or her hand.

"How many knew him as Ross Hollifield?" I asked. Most of them raised their hands again. "Which picture did they recognize? Anybody?"

"Chief," Jan Smitty, one of the two female detectives from Knox County spoke. "They all knew him as the toothless hayseed, wherever I went. Nobody recognized the hippie-looking picture or Rosenbaum as himself. He's got this identity pretty well established.

"Most people view him as an outsider — which I take is how they view everyone not born here — but he's the kind of outsider they like. He spends money locally and doesn't bother anyone."

"Thanks, Smitty. Anybody else get a different take?"

"The guy at the hardware told me that he thought maybe ol' Ross cooks a little meth up there, but had no real grounds for believing it, other than the fact that he's secretive," Al Reagan said.

"Hollifield attends the little Pentecostal Church down on Highway 33 enough for the preacher to comment that 'Brother Ross' shares the bounty of his money with God. I'm beginning to wonder if this guy *is* Rosenbaum."

"If it isn't Rosenbaum, Ross Hollifield is going to get a scare like he's probably never had before — and an official apology from us. But I believe it's him. He told me he'd had years to prepare. Anybody else want to share?"

"Chief, I talked to one of Hollifield's neighbor's at the little supermarket in Maynardville. She said that there was a truck-load of fertilizer delivered to the Hollifield place a couple of months ago, but he's never plowed a furrow since he's been there." The speaker was Tiff Kirby, the other female detective with us.

"It hasn't showed on any of the aerial photos, so that means it's covered. It only took a truck load of the right kind of fertilizer to take down the federal building in Oklahoma City. And the same stuff is still for sale on the open market. Good information, Kirby."

Everyone turned as an unmarked black van pulled into the lot.

"Here are the last two members of our team," I said.

The black van stopped in a small cloud of dust and a short, stocky man of perhaps forty, wearing a base ball cap that said **BOMB TECH**, then in small letters *If you see me running, try to stay ahead.*

"How's it going, Mitch?" I met him with outstretched hand.

"What's up, Shiloh, my man? Don't stick that hand out, give me a hug." We embraced clumsily as Southern males do, and the other officers watched with obvious curiosity.

"Ladies and gentlemen," I said, "this old reprobate is Mitch Cleland. We went to school together at Glynco a few years ago."

"Didn't know you'd trained at Glynco, Chief," Jan Smitty said.

"There's probably a lot you don't know about this old geezer," Mitch said. "I woulda made a real warrior out of him but he was too interested in becoming a rich novelist."

"What agency are you with?" John Freed asked.

"If I told you, I'd have to kill every one of you," Mitch said. "So let's let it go at that. Besides, I'm just here to babysit Mister Talon." He went over and opened the sliding door on the side of his unmarked van.

The officers all gathered around to look at the device in the back of the van. "It's a robot," someone said.

"It's a Foster-Miller TALON robot," Tiff Kirby said. "It can go just about anywhere and carry anything. I heard that one fell off a truck in Iraq and sunk in the river. Supposedly they started it remotely and *drove* it out of the water."

"Give the young woman a gold star," Mitch said. "This particular one is just for recon, but these devices can do a remarkable number of things."

"Golly, how much does one of those things cost?" Freed asked.

"*Golly?* Haven't you taught this guy to cuss like a cop, Tempest?"

"John is a gentleman," I said.

"Let's just say that nobody here will be buying even a stripped down Mister Talon in the near future, John," Mitch said.

"All right, B Team over there," I said. "Everyone in vests, a shotgun for every two officers, and as many in one car as you can comfortably fit. The Union County officers will guide you to the old logging road. Remember, nobody closer than two hundred yards without a go ahead. Al, radio when you're all in position. Be careful."

"You be careful, too, Chief. Let's move out," Reagan said.

"We'll give them a few minutes head start," I said. "They have to walk through a wooded area to get in place. Is your machine ready to deploy as soon as we get there, Mitch?"

"All I have to do is unload it and turn it on. What kind of terrain will my little buddy be covering?

"It's gravel driveway, up a small grade then downhill — about two football fields distance. How long will it take the robot to go that far?"

"It will go a lot faster than the speed I'll be using. I can cover that much distance in twenty minutes without a lot of trouble. Do we know anything about alarm systems or cameras?'

"I'm assuming there'll be both, but there was no way to check closely without tipping him off. We found out today that a truckload of fertilizer went in there and disappeared from sight. I'm assuming Rosenbaum will be heavily armed. He was making silencers and converting weapons to full automatic in his basement."

"Rosenbaum? Tim Rosenbaum? That's who we're going after?'

"Haven't you been reading the newspaper or watching television the last month?"

"No, I've been in Afghanistan. I know that *greasy* bastard Rosenbaum, though. He was in a class I taught on bombs about five years ago. I had to take him to the woodshed about sexually harassing an agent in the class."

"Small woman, waif-like?" I asked.

"Yeah. How did you know?"

"It's his pattern. He murdered a girl in her apartment a couple of years ago. He escaped custody after we took him down."

"Cynthia Quinn. I remember. I don't like him, Shiloh, but he knows his stuff. If he's rigged his place to blow, it may be one hell of an explosion."

"That's why I asked for the favor, Mitch. I know he's capable of anything."

"Let's roll, then," Mitch said.

I rode with Mitch, and by the time we reached the driveway on Beard Valley, Al Reagan had radioed that his team was in place. We strung the vehicles along the road, except for the van, which Mitch backed into the driveway so he could see his monitors as he guided the robot in. The only sound when the TALON robot began to move was the gravel being crunched by the tracks, which are a miniature version of what you see on a bulldozer or tank.

"Team B, we're sending the 'bot in. Has there been any movement?"

"No movement from the Team B side," Al said.

"Eagle's Nest, any movement?"

"A white male walked from the housetrailer down to the concrete building and went in two hours ago. The old pickup truck is still in place. No movement since then."

"Ten-four, Eagle's Nest and Team B, hold your positions."

The robot gave a remarkably clear picture as it rumbled slowly over the hill, then started down. At the foot of the hill, Mitch Cleland swiveled the cameras, scanning the housetrailer and the concrete building. Up close, it looked exactly like a bunker from a World War II movie. It appeared that most of it was underground with a staircase leading to what appeared to be a steel door.

"Nobody in sight. Let's take a look behind the bunker." The robot started moving again but after a few feet the screen was filled with a white flash.

"Oh hell," Mitch said, "something just blew."

The sound of a small explosion hit our ears, and seconds later another explosion made a thunderous roar that was deafening and sent a mushroom pillar of debris and smoke into the air fifty feet or more above the hill protecting us. For a moment the bizarre idea that Rosenbaum had a nuclear weapon crossed my mind. As the blast died down, small debris began to rain all over us.

"Team B, report!" I said into the radio.

"We're good," Al Reagan said. "We were all behind the embankment but there's debris falling all over the place."

"Eagle's Nest, what do you see from your position?"

"The bunker is gone and there's a big crater. The trailer is scattered across the field. That was a *big* explosion, Chief."

"He's right, Shiloh. I would say we now know where the truck load of fertilizer went and that it was ammonium nitrate," Mitch said. "As a bomb maker, he was talented. It looks like most of the blast was focused on the bunker — maximum damage, limited range."

"Hey, Mister Cleland," John Freed yelled at Mitch.

"Yeah, Boy Scout?"

"I think you're going to need a new robot."

"You're right, Boy Scout. I think we could have used Rosenbaum in Afghanistan," Mitch said.

Sam Renfro and I stood on the perimeter of what had been Tim Rosenbaum's bunker the morning after the explosion, just after the hazardous material teamed had certified the area safe, and watched the arson investigators sift through the fragments of concrete that were left, searching for his remains. What they had found, bone fragments and bits of flesh, had fit in small bags. Two of our forensics people were bagging the evidence as it was found.

"Shiloh, if you hadn't done it the way you did yesterday, casualties would have been over twenty police officers who are still breathing today," the Sheriff said. "Rosenbaum went out with a bang."

"If I had confronted him when I had my first suspicions, he might have just left the department rather than face the investigation."

"You don't know that, Shiloh. Besides, there's absolutely no way to know what he would have done in the future. He was a man at war with the universe."

"All three of the three basic plots rolled into one," I said, "an individual in conflict with other individuals, himself and the forces of nature."

"*What?*" Sam asked, looking at me with an expression of doubt in his face, as if he thought I might have cracked.

"Nothing important, Sam. I just remembered something someone once told me."

One of the arson investigators approached us, holding something in his hand. "Do either of you know if Rosenbaum had all his teeth?"

"He had partial in front," I said. "It was an upper plate, front teeth."

"That would explain *this*," he said, holding up a shiny, twisted piece of metal. We looked closer and saw that there were two teeth attached to it, now pointing in opposite directions.

"Give it to one of the forensic technicians. Rosenbaum's dentist will be able to tell us if it belonged to him," I said.

"*If* it belonged to him, Shiloh? Do you have any doubt that he blew himself up yesterday afternoon?" Sam asked.

"Sam, there's no body. To satisfy me, I would need to drive a stake through his heart, and the arson investigators found an escape tunnel that came out just inside the edge of the woods."

"You've been under a lot of stress, Shiloh. Hell, we *all* have. We'll have DNA run on the remains we have, but *I'm* satisfied that he's gone," Sam said.

"Run his DNA against *what*, Sam? When we were searching his house, we were focused on the guns, manuals and silencers. Nobody recovered a hair brush or a toothbrush because we thought everything would be there if we needed it. Rosenbaum burned that house while we weren't looking."

"We'll find a relative," Sam said.

"His mother and father are dead, no siblings. If he has relatives, they're somewhere in Michigan where his parents moved from nearly forty years ago."

Sam was quiet for a moment.

"All right, we'll run the DNA we've collected through all the databases and try to prove it *wasn't* someone else. I'm satisfied, though. Blowing himself up and taking everyone with him — which is what he had planned, not expecting the robot — is just the kind of thing a sick fuck like him would do. Lighten up, Hoss. It's over and the good guys won."

TWENTY-FOUR

In the mid-seventeenth century Anton van Leeuwenhoek, a Dutch merchant who sold cloth for a living, became fascinated with the lenses used to count threads in fabric. He began to grind his own lenses, finally producing one that could magnify an object more than two-hundred times. One day, he put a drop of water under his lens and saw a world populated with fantastic monsters he referred to as *animalcules.*

Leeuwenhoek was not the first man to peer through a lens that magnified tiny objects but he was the first to make detailed drawings of what he saw. Until he showed them differently, even scholars believed that creatures such as larvae were spontaneously generated from the substance in which they were found. Without a day of university training, he was made a fellow of the Royal Society of England, and became one of the most famous scientists of his times.

I've always wondered, though, if Leeuwenhoek ever enjoyed a cool, seemingly clear drink of water again after he looked through that lens and discovered there were tiny monsters floating around. It's a peculiar thought, I suppose. But after a person deals with enough monsters, it affects the way he or she thinks about everything.

Most people in civilized countries are insulated from real evil, or see it in palatable form on television or in films. The majority, unless they are unlucky enough to become a victim of the truly evil, convince themselves that it is the stuff of fiction with no concrete application to their humdrum day-to-day lives.

Police officers lose that innocence. Like Anton van Leeuwenhoek, they know that monstrous creatures exist, though not evident to the naked eye. They fear for their loved ones in a way that sometimes becomes destructive and smothering. It's that fear that breaks up most cop marriages, not alcohol or drugs or adultery. It's the fear.

In the month that had elapsed since the explosion that Rosenbaum had intended to kill those who came after him, we had learned things. The TALON robot had set off one of several small explosives devices buried just under the surface. Each small explosive had been set to detonate everything else when it went off.

The twisted partial plate found in the debris had been identified by Rosenbaum's dentist as the one he had fitted for the former chief of detectives. Only the remnants of two rifles had been found after the explosion, which meant that Rosenbaum had lied to me or had another cache of weapons somewhere.

We ran the DNA from the human remains found at the destroyed bunker and it was not in any database that we could find. Everyone was satisfied that Tim Rosenbaum had died in the explosion. It was the only logical conclusion. Still, the only thing I could think of was the escape tunnel, though there was no evidence that he had used it.

When a seventy-three year old former captain for whom Rosenbaum and I had both worked died in his front yard a week after the explosion, I was suspicious. He had been sitting in a lawn chair and his wife had seen him stand suddenly and walk towards the house, collapsing a few feet from the door.

I asked his wife if we could have an autopsy performed and she said absolutely not. I told the Sheriff I wanted to get a court order because the captain had once dressed then-Sergeant Rosenbaum down in front of the entire detachment.

"Damn, Shiloh! Captain Hurst was an old man with a bad heart, diabetes and emphysema. His wife doesn't want an autopsy and I'm not going to put her through it," Sam said.

I read up on nicotine poisoning and found out all the fatal symptoms that even a small amount of the substance introduced directly into the body could cause. Rosenbaum had a formula for nicotine poison to dip tiny darts in. A small dart might easily have fallen out during resuscitation attempts and transport. Even Jennifer suggested that I might need counseling when I discussed *that* theory with her.

Sam asked me to stay on as chief of detectives until he could decide on a replacement to fill the slot, and I agreed. Despite the nagging fear, my impotence of body and soul had not returned. I was even writing again, fitfully at first, like a man recovering from a broken leg learns to walk again, but gaining ground every day.

Rosenbaum's story had been picked up by the national news media. The Sheriff had respected my wishes and did not insist that I be interviewed. I had been offered a sizeable advance to write a book on the case, but I turned it down. The entire event was still too raw to put on paper.

These thoughts were all bubbling in my head as I carried a bag of groceries from Ingles supermarket to my department Chevrolet compact on a sunny day in early June. I drove home, taking my time, and as I approached my driveway, a pickup truck towing a riding lawn mower was pulling away from the house next door. As I turned into my driveway, it took me a few seconds to realize that my own lawn was freshly mowed as well as the yard next door.

Puzzled, I walked across the yard and knocked on the next-door neighbor's storm door. Lydia Hammond, a widow in her early seventies, opened it a moment later, drying her hands on a dish towel. Lydia is one of those women whose faces hold on to their youthful beauty, not so much aging as adding character — as I expect Jennifer to age.

"Shiloh, how nice to see you. Won't you come in?"

"Actually, Lydia, I have groceries in the car. I was just wondering if you could tell me who mowed my lawn."

"I can do better than that, Shiloh. He left a card for you. Just a minute." She retreated into the house and came back with a card that said: "Franklin's Lawn Service," with a telephone number.

"He came by this afternoon and asked if I had a regular lawn service. I told him, I didn't and he said he's do it for thirty-five dollars. When he was finished, he came back and asked if I knew if *you* had a regular service. I told him I didn't think so. He said he was going to do a complimentary job for you since he was already here, and if you like the work, you can call him and he'll put both of us on the same schedule."

"Thanks, Lydia. You're looking good as always."

"You flatter an old lady, Shiloh. How's that beautiful Jennifer doing?"

"She's doing well. I stopped at the grocery store and bought a roast chicken for dinner and I'm going to make pasta and a salad."

"Jen's a lucky girl. I also had a husband who liked to do things in the kitchen," Lydia said. "A *real* man who didn't worry what others thought."

"Now *you're* the one doing the flattering," I said with a smile.

I walked around the house once. Everything looked like it was in place and the guy had done a good job mowing. Inside the house, I punched the alarm system code in and put the groceries on the table. I picked up the phone and dialed the number for Franklin's Lawn Service off the card Lydia had given me.

"Hello," a friendly female voice said, "you have reached Franklin's Yard Service. We're not available to take your call. Please leave a message at the tone and we'll get back to you as soon as possible."

I hung up the phone because I don't like talking to machines. I put the card in my wallet and decided I'd call him back later. We needed a lawn service. The hot sun isn't good for my health and Jen never has time for mowing. It would be nice to have the grass cut regularly without having to track down and hire a neighborhood kid, who would usually do a sloppy job.

From the grocery bag I removed the Roma tomatoes, red and green bell peppers and a large cucumber. I washed them, sliced them, and put them in a salad bowl. I opened a bottle of ginger salad dressing and drizzled it over the vegetables. I covered the salad bowl with plastic wrap and shook it to mix the salad, then put it in the refrigerator to chill.

Removing a large platter from an overhead cabinet, I sliced the roasted chicken and covered it with plastic wrap. The sliced chicken joined the salad in the refrigerator. I looked at my watch, and put on water for my angel hair pasta. I timed it perfectly because Jennifer is punctual. By the time she came in, I was setting the table.

She stopped just inside the door, stepped out of her shoes, paused to look at the table and smiled. "He's handsome, a great lover and he cooks. I think I'll keep him."

A moment later, my beautiful Latina lady was kissing me warmly and deeply. She paused and leaned back to look in my eyes.

"Is boudoir service on the menu for the night?" she asked.

"I could probably be persuaded. You're cheerful today," I said.

"As well I should be. I won my appeal on the Josie Fletcher case. The District Attorney has agreed to a manslaughter plea rather than try the case again. I was going to take us out for a celebration, but I like what I see. We'll just eat in."

"I'll try to rise to the occasion," I said.

"That's not a problem you have these days — rising to the occasion."

"You always have been a brazen wench," I said.

We kissed again, then washed our hands for dinner. Forty minutes later, she rinsed the last dish and I put them in the dishwasher.

"Would you care to join me in a shower, Chief?"

She walked slowly down the hall dropping items of clothing, casting glances over her shoulder. By the time we reached the bathroom, she was naked and I was half-skipping, getting undressed, moving awkwardly across the carpet.

As the hot water poured over us, we soaped each other sensually. When I grew too insistent, she said, "Back off a little, Tiger. I want a distance run tonight, not a sprint."

We dried each other off with the amazingly soft Egyptian cotton towels I had splurged on when we were in New York on a book tour, and I followed her to the bed, watching the sensuous rise and fall of her hips.

By the time we tumbled into bed, it was she who had become insistent and I who held back until I could hold no longer, and we merged into one person, ending with a series of gasps and moans from deep in Jen's body.

Afterwards, we lay for a few minutes, basking in the afterglow. She trailed her fingers lightly up and down my chest, touching the scar from coronary bypass surgery.

"You're pretty good for the sick, pathetic old man you thought you were just a few weeks ago. Adrenalin agrees with you, Chief," she said.

"The incentive is everything," I replied.

Jen sat up in the bed. "Have your cigarette. I left my cell phone in my jacket pocket somewhere in the kitchen. I'll be right back."

I watched with admiration as she padded away on bare feet, and lit a cigarette. I took a deep drag and thought how good life really is when a man is living it, not just waiting to die. Then I heard Jennifer scream.

I grabbed the .44 Charter Arms Bulldog from the nightstand where I had been keeping it for the last month, and ran down the hall to the kitchen.

"There was a man at the back door, tinkering with the lock," Jen said, shaking with fear. "He ran when I screamed."

I pushed back the curtain and looked out on the back porch. "You scared him away. Go get my robe, please."

While she was gone, I got my flashlight from the drawer where I kept it, watching the door for shadows. When she brought my robe, I put it on and stepped out on the porch barefooted and played the light around the back yard, pistol in hand. When I turned to go back in, I stepped on something cold and metallic. I picked it up and carried it inside, locking the door behind me.

In the living room, I turned on the light. Jennifer was sitting on the couch, still shivering from time to time. "What did you find?" she asked.

"It's a pick from a professional lock-picking kit," I said, holding it in the light.

"He must be a brazen burglar," she said. "It's still early and we had lights on."

"Professional home burglars don't break into houses at night. It's too dangerous and there's enhanced jail time. Business burglaries are done at night. Professional home burglars usually work between ten in the morning and three in the afternoon, when people are out. Only a junkie would be wired enough to break into an occupied house and junkies kick in doors or break windows. They don't use lock picks.

"What I want to know is why the alarm system didn't work," I said.

The next morning, I called my office and told them I'd be late. Ed Bergman had arrived just a few minutes after Jennifer left for work. I walked with him around the house. He carried a stepladder and checked each individual piece of equipment.

"Everything's good out here," he said. "Let's go inside."

"How about a cup of coffee, Ed? I made a pot right before you got here."

"Sure. With a little milk, if you have it."

As I poured the coffee, one sugar for me and a little milk for Ed, he took the cover off the keypad and peered into it. "Shiloh, have you been tinkering with this?"

"Ed, I can't remember which way a bolt turns from one time to the next. I know nothing about things with electronic circuits."

"How about Jennifer? Women are bad to tinker with thermostats and things like that. Do you think she may have let curiosity get the best of her?"

"I don't think so."

"Well, somebody has tinkered with it. The interface between the keypad and the main system has been switched off. All the right lights are on, but it's like disconnecting the brain from the body. There's no communication between them."

"How much trouble was it to change?" I asked.

He inserted a small screwdriver into the exposed keypad and there was a tiny click. "Hardly any trouble if you know what you're doing. I just fixed it."

"Ed, are you certain it was working right when you installed it?"

"Shiloh, I know my business. I set the alarm off several times, testing the system."

"I didn't mean to imply otherwise, Ed. But the alternative explanation is that someone managed to unlock the door and disable the system before the alarm went off."

"It would take someone with a key, or someone who was a locksmith *and* knew alarm systems inside out. You know anybody like that?" Ed asked.

"I did, but he's supposed to be dead."

"Well, it's working now, but if there's somebody as good as he'd have to be wants in here, what you've got now won't keep him out."

"It would appear that way," I said. "I'm going to pack clothes and toiletries for Jen to stay somewhere else for awhile, and if this guy comes back, I'll be waiting. In the meantime, put a good man on the house during daylight hours— and actually send me a bill this time, Ed. This is getting too expensive for a favor."

"I'll have somebody here before you're finished packing, Shiloh. We'll settle up when this is over," Ed told me.

TWENTY-FIVE

Ralph Waldo Emerson once wrote 'The wise man in the storm prays to God, not for safety from danger, but deliverance from fear.' He was right. Every courageous person knows that the fear vanishes once action begins.

The five days following the prowler at my house, the discovery that someone had violated the sanctity of my home was one long period of fear, a gut-wrenching fear that tightened the muscles of my back and caused me to silently pray for deliverance. It was doubly hard going through the days without confiding in any of my friends.

Any one of my friends and associates would have volunteered to act as round-the-clock bodyguard for me and Jennifer, but I knew there was only one ending possible and it required waiting. Bodyguards and security measures would only prolong my agony.

John Kennedy knew when he was president, with the Secret Service surrounding him, that a determined assassin could not be stopped. He knew there was no way that even the best security detail ever assembled could stop a man with a rifle. Every cop, in his or her deepest being, knows that *anybody* can be taken down if the assassin is willing to pay the price.

I had no fear, however, of rifles or even bombs because I was certain that my stalker wanted me up close and personal, and that the quickest way to make the fear go away was to wait, no matter how long it took. I was on his schedule, not mine. So I had been working long hours, trying to keep my mind occupied.

All the detectives who worked in the squad room had gone for the night. The cleaning crew was already at work. A petite black woman, whose I name I had learned was Mary, had come through emptying wastebaskets. When she came into my office to empty my basket into a barrel she pushed around, she was always shy, but friendly.

"How are you tonight, Mary?"

"I'm fine, Chief. I see you're working late again. This is four nights in a row. Don't your wife get put out wit' your long hours."

"She doesn't care for it much, but she knows it's just for a while."

After she left, I was surprised to see Al Reagan come through the squad room door, coat across his shoulder and tie loosened. He came to my office door.

"Why are you here so late?" I asked. "It's not good for a marriage."

"You should talk. I had some paperwork to catch up. I'm going to Waffle House for my cholesterol fix. You want to go?"

"No, I'm tired. I'll be heading home in a few minutes." *To set up aluminum pie plates in front of all the doors and sleep sitting up in a chair with a gun in my hand, so that I will hopefully awaken in time to get my shadow stalker before he gets me*, I thought but did not say.

"All right, Chief. I'll see you tomorrow."

"Hey, Al," I said as he turned to leave, "would you and John like to move out of that cramped room where you're working and join everyone else?"

"We kind of like it back there, Shiloh."

"Would you like to be a lieutenant, Al? There's an opening. Robison has asked to go back to patrol."

"Let me think about it, Shiloh. I don't like being chained to a desk."

"Good night, Al."

"Good night, Shiloh... oh, excuse me, I didn't see you." Al had nearly collided with one of the janitorial staff, a tall, stooped man with stringy blond hair sticking in all directions from under his baseball cap. He had a colored lens on the left side of his glasses, like those usually worn by people who are blind in one eye. I saw that he had a pronounced limp as he pushed the floor buffer to the back of the squad room and unwound the cord to plug it in.

In my office, I took out the card that said *Franklin's Lawn Service* and dialed the number from my desk phone. The man with the buffer stiffened when his cell phone began to ring, then became still. By that time, I was standing in a firing position with my baby Glock pistol centered on his back.

"*Touché*, Shiloh," he said, raising his hands in the air without turning around.

"So, we're back to first names now, Timmy?"

"Don't be insulting, Shiloh. We've come too far for pettiness. I'm not even angry with you any longer."

"And yet you still came here to kill me?"

"Well, that's true, Shiloh. But I'm not angry. You liberated me from counting ceiling tiles and putting everything in the proper order on shelves, and from recording everything I eat and keeping track of bowel movements.

"It's exhilarating out here on the edge. I've fucked three petite young girls since you set me free from my restraints. Watching the fear in their eyes was *delicious*. As far as I know, none of them even called the police."

"If you're not angry, then *why?*"

"You were the only opponent worthy enough to frustrate my plans, Shiloh. I was amazed at how well you put together the sequence of events before and after I killed Cynthia Quinn.

"You had it all right except for thinking I took her keys from the purse the day I met her. As you know by now, I don't *need* keys. How did you know I killed her, Shiloh?"

"It was just good police work, nothing more, Timmy."

"Oh come now. We both know better than that. What caused your mind to go in that direction in the first place?"

"I really don't know, and it doesn't matter because it ends here, Timmy."

"Yes, I suppose it will end here. But *how* will it end, Shiloh? May I turn around?"

"How it ends will depend entire on you, Timmy. I'm a cop, not an executioner. Keep your hands up and turn very slowly," I said.

"Let's *not* play games, Shiloh," he said, turning slowly to face me. "You know how you *want* it to end. Otherwise, you would have called dispatch on your phone instead of me, or you would have stepped the few feet to the door and called for help.

"Now you've committed the cop's cardinal sin of letting me turn around, knowing full well that if I reach for my weapon and you miss or fail to disable me with the first rounds, I may get off some rounds, too.

"I'm taking off my glasses, slowly with my right hand. I'll let them drop to the floor. Don't get trigger happy, Shiloh, I'm enjoying our talk." The glasses dropped with a loud, metallic clink.

His face was still Tim Rosenbaum, but a distorted Tim Rosenbaum, looking through eyes that were totally malevolent and devoid of all humanity. A reptile's eyes.

"Who died in your homemade bunker?" I asked.

"A man of no consequence. A drunk I hired in Mechanicsville to help me with the physical labor of building my sanctuary. I bought him cheap vodka by the case. He stayed drunk and slept in the trailer, so I kept him around in case I needed him. As it turned out, I did

"By the way, how did you find me?" he asked.

"You left data on your laptop computer," I replied.

"So much for professional grade software."

"Who told you we were coming?" I asked.

"The first call came from the little Pentecostal preacher whose palm I greased well on Sundays as Ross Hollifield. The second was from the hardware store. It's a small community and they don't trust outsiders at all, Shiloh. You should have known that." He tried to smile, but a twisted grimace was all he could manage.

"I don't suppose it mattered to you at all that you planned to kill men and women who had worked for you for years?" I said.

"I might have before you liberated me, Shiloh. But not afterwards. You already have a lot of blood on your conscience, and a conscience is a handicap," he said, gazing straight into my eyes.

"Did you kill Captain Hurst?"

"Yes, I did. It went just as I planned. The tiny nicotine-coated dart was lost when they were moving him around, but I knew you'd figure it out because I promised *you* an old, dead cop."

"Why didn't you just kill me with one of your silenced .22 caliber pistols tonight? You obviously moved them before we got there."

"Shiloh, killing you with a pistol would have been pedestrian. I was going to slit your throat and watch your eyes while you were bleeding out."

"That's why I have the pistol pointed at *you* now, Timmy. A weapon is just a tool for me, like a hammer or a saw. I never took any pleasure in watching people suffer, but I knew you'd come after me like this if I waited long enough."

"I'd planned to do it in your own house, then rape Jennifer. She's not my type, but after watching *her* watch *you* die, I could have managed. She really is beautiful, in a peasant sort of way. I watched the two of you when you came out of the shower," he said.

My finger twitched on the trigger, but I held back because I *am* a cop, not an executioner, But holding a pistol at the ready is a strain, even in training exercises. It had to end soon.

"Ah, that last reference to your beloved wet-back bitch almost did it. You *wanted* to pull the trigger. You also want to think we're different. But we're not. You love the violence as much as I do. You just haven't admitted it yet."

Mary from the cleaning crew pushed open the squad room door to turn off the lights because she thought I was gone, but I didn't know this until later. I was totally focused on Tim Rosenbaum's eyes. As the door opened, his eyes moved, as the eyes always move before the body moves.

I put two rounds in his chest and one through his forehead, before his hand could reach his waistband. He probably died almost instantly, but I edged forward, pistol still trained on him. Mary was screaming, but I didn't really hear her. I saw that a stake through the heart would not be needed.

EPILOG

Suspension with pay, pending investigation is the rule at the sheriff's department and most law enforcement agencies these days. I was also encouraged to spend time with a department psychologist, but I didn't.

By the fifth day after the shooting, Jen and I had fallen into a routine. I stayed home and prepared gourmet meals and listened to Warren Zevon and Steve Earle, sometimes wishing that Warren had not left the world at the age fifty-six. We were the same age and it would have been nice to see what kind of music he produced at sixty. But all things happen in their own time.

Jennifer called me at least three times a day to check on me, and so did Sam Renfro and Al Reagan, who always told me that John Freed said, "Hey." The official investigation had been completed quickly, and I knew my continued suspension was Sam's way of letting me rest.

Tim Rosenbaum had been armed, not with a silenced .22 but with his .40 caliber service Glock and a Loveless boot knife worth a thousand dollars, with which he had intended to cut my throat. Those facts were not in dispute.

It was what cops call "a clean shoot," as if there is such a thing as the clean killing of a human being. Only I knew that I had killed Tim Rosenbaum *before* his hand moved towards the weapon. What if I had misjudged the movement of his eyes? Was he right in his assessment that I had engineered the situation so that I could kill him instead of sending him to the penitentiary?

Had my fear and rage turned me into a murderer, no better than Tim Rosenbaum? In my heart, I knew that even locked away at Brushy Mountain or Riverbed, Tim Rosenbaum would have been plotting my death and injury to those I loved because of his hatred for me, which despite what he said, had become all consuming. Would I have ever been free of the fear as long as he lived?

That's why on the sixth day after the shooting I drove to the hospital where I had received my defibrillator and made inquiries at the security office. I found the man I was looking for sitting quietly in the chapel. He turned as I entered.

"Ah, Mister Tempest. How did you know where to find me?"

"A guy with a gun and a badge told me you're always here at this time of day, Father Fleming."

"I meant to visit you again, after I revisited some theology texts, but things were busy and you were released before I got back. You've been busy since we last talked. Most of it made the newspapers. How can I help you?" he asked.

"I really don't know. I came over here thinking I might ask you to hear my confession, but now that I'm here, I don't think so," I said.

"The last time we talked, you weren't too sure of God's existence"

"I'm still not totally sure of God's existence," I said.

"An honest answer," he said. "But of course, you're an honest man, not a hypocrite."

"Isn't there something in the Bible about, 'I believe, but help my unbelief,'" I asked.

"Yes, it was Mark 9:24; the father of a demon possessed child said that."

"Did you know that Saint Cornelius, a Roman Centurion who sent for Simon Peter and whose family became the first Gentiles to receive the Holy Spirit and who was later ordained a bishop, was more of a police officer than a soldier? Probably a man not unlike yourself."

"I read that somewhere," I said.

"If you *had* come to confess, what would you have confessed?" Father Fleming asked.

"I killed another human being."

"If you had said that to me, I would have asked if it was it in self-defense or defense of another. The prohibition is against murder, not justified killing. The newspaper said it was clearly self-defense. You are, after all, a police officer entrusted with the power of lethal force."

"Internal affairs and the District Attorney General say it was self-defense," I said. "I'll suffer no legal penalty for having killed him."

"So the only person not convinced that the killing was justified is you?" he said.

"That's about the size of it. I keep asking myself if I deliberately let things go to the point where I had to kill him because I *wanted* to kill him and make the world safe for other people, especially the woman I love and myself."

"Shiloh... do you mind if I call you Shiloh?"

"Not at all, Father Fleming."

"As I see it, Shiloh, you want *absolution*, but not the confession that precedes it. That's not possible. I can't absolve you of a sin you aren't sure you committed. If you had come in here and said you arranged to kill him with deliberation, I could absolve you after an honest confession. But if you don't know whether you committed murder, I can't offer absolution."

"I thought priests had to understand right and wrong with a certainty."

"No, my friend. That isn't true. A priest merely takes your word as to whether you have sinned. You have to know first whether you have committed a sin that needs absolution," the priest said. "At that point, you confess and receive absolution."

"Well, then I'm sorry to have taken up your time. And I'm sorry I was rude and arrogant when you came to visit before."

"Now *that* I can take care of. *I* forgive you for being rude and arrogant to me. I sensed that you were in an emotional storm and I see a lot of posturing in such cases. Your celebrity status and intellect intimidated me, and I didn't do *my* job."

"Thank you," I said.

"If it's any comfort, Shiloh, there are men and women who can never be satisfied with absolution because they distrust their own motives. Many of them are priests."

"Who will watch the watchers, in an extreme version," I said.

"Something like that," he replied.

I nodded and turned to leave, but he spoke again.

"Shiloh, would you like to get a beer and talk a while?" the priest asked. "Maybe you can tell me what happened, bounce a few things off me. Maybe you'll even absolve yourself before we're finished talking."

"It's worth a shot," I said, feeling strangely elated. "Drinks on me."

"Of course they are. I'm under a vow of poverty, and a cheapskate to boot."

"Do you read a lot of murder mysteries, Father?

"If we're going to drink together, you'll have to call me by my given name. It's Ethan," he said. "And now that you mention it, I do. On page one-hundred-twenty-seven of *The Underbelly*, you had James pick up his pistol and put it in his pocket — but he had already put it in his pocket on page one-twenty-five."

"Everybody's a critic," I said as we left the chapel.

About the Author

David Hunter is a decorated former police officer, a 23-year editorial columnist for the *Knoxville News-Sentinel*, author of 18 books—novels, memoirs, and true crime. His awards include the Knoxville Writers' Guild 2008 Career Achievement Award. He was nominated for an Edgar for his first mystery novel, *The Jigsaw Man*, the Appalachian Writers Best Book Award for *The Archangel Caper*, and was named a member of The Writers Hall of Fame by the East Tennessee Friends of the Library.

His work has appeared in *Mad*, *Reader's Digest*, and elsewhere. His latest novel is *Tempest and the Infinite Variations*, a police procedural set in Knoxville, where he lives with his wife, his son, his German shepherd, and three cockatiels.

CPSIA information can be obtained at www.ICGtesting.com
Printed in the USA
LVOW07s0226151114

413713LV00002B/169/P